I0552850

DARKENED DESTINIES

Also by Gary Lee Vincent

Novels
PASSAGEWAY
BELLY TIMBER
ATTACK OF THE MELONHEADS

Darkened—The West Virginia Vampire Series
DARKENED HILLS
DARKENED HOLLOWS
DARKENED WATERS
DARKENED SOULS
DARKENED MINDS

Nonfiction
THE WINNER, THE LOSER
AGELATIONS
CONFIGURATION MANAGEMENT

Musical Releases
100 PERCENT
PASSION, PLEASURE, & PAIN
SOMEWHERE DOWN THE ROAD

DARKENED DESTINIES

GARY LEE VINCENT

Burning Bulb
PUBLISHING

Darkened Destinies
By **Gary Lee Vincent**

Burning Bulb Publishing
P.O. Box 4721
Bridgeport, WV 26330-4721
www.BurningBulbPublishing.com

PUBLISHER'S NOTE: This book is a work of fiction. Names, characters, places, and incidents are either the product of the author's imagination or are used fictitiously, and any resemblance to actual persons, living or dead, events, or locales is purely coincidental.

Copyright © 2017 Gary Lee Vincent. All rights reserved.
Cover model Dante Heks.

Edition ISBN

Paperback 978-1-948278-01-0

First edition.
Printed in the United States of America.

PART 1

THE BLOODLESS MISSING PERSON'S TRAIL

CHAPTER 1

Police Officer Susan Lafitte wrenched the crusty bread roll from her mouth and chewed the huge bite she'd taken, her eyes fixed on the seated figure of William McConnellson III, just visible through the small one-way glass panel into the interview room. The young man sat with his head in his hands, his long, lean arms resting his elbows on the gray table.

Lafitte's young police colleague, Dwayne Cooley stared at her, boggle-eyed. "We gotta let him go?" he asked, incredulously. "But he's the only suspect we got!"

Lafitte chomped with her mouth full, her speech barely intelligible through a spray of breadcrumbs and meat that exploded from her mouth with every word. "Makes no difference!"

It reminded Cooley of the scene that day they picked up McConnellson. Brain matter. Blobs of flesh. Gobbets of fat. He'd imagined it all flying through the air in the frenzied attack.

But Lafitte was still spitting it all out as she spoke: "No matter. We've kept him for the maximum time and we got no real evidence."

Cooley wiped a wet crumb from his cheek. "But we found the guy right at the scene!"

His stomach rolled at the terrifying memory of the room in which they had found the young man, and the gory sight of Donovan Smith's murder scene. The victim hadn't simply been torn limb from limb, but had been shredded into pieces in a manic attack, resulting in an explosion of flesh in which tiny lumps of fat, gristle and bone had covered almost every surface—including the ceiling and all four walls. Officer Cooley would never forget the cooked pork aroma—apparently coming from the chunks of flesh burning on the hot, illuminated light bulbs where they had landed. Instinctively, in a reflex action that had horrified him, he had actually salivated at the smell—before his gag reflex kicked in and he'd ended up puking.

Cooley watched Susan Lafitte's teeth churning her huge bite of baloney sandwich in her open mouth as she struggled to eat, breathe and talk all at once. Pink meat, yellow grease and white mush rolled around her blood-red tongue. Cooley gulped down a throatful of rising bile.

"As you recall," Lafitte chewed, then swallowed hard, and pointed the half-eaten sandwich at him, continuing to speak with a thankfully empty mouth, now: "…Dwayne. There was no blood at the scene to speak of. How could a guy like that have torn a body apart, and got no blood on him, whatsoever? It don't stand to reason. It's impossible."

Cooley shrugged his narrow shoulders. "Maybe he killed him someplace else? Drained him like a slit-throated hog, some other place, then brought him back home?"

3

The female officer gave him a quizzical look, one bushy eyebrow raised. "What? And then blew up the body all over the guy's room with a stick of dynamite or something?"

"I don't know!" Cooley gasped, exasperated.

***

William McConnellson III's mind had been working overtime, stuck in there for hours—days? He'd lost count. *I don't think they can keep me for longer than three days without charging me, can they?* he thought. So, it must have been fewer than three days, he concluded, since no one had charged him with murder yet, nor a lesser crime. Although…who knew if the law applied these days, in these crazy times?

God help us all! Will implored, raising his eyes to the ceiling, as if Heaven lay somewhere inside the stained polystyrene tiles and florescent strip-light above his head. In all honesty, Will didn't know if God listened anymore. It was hard to believe, after the sights Will had seen and the things he'd had to do, in his short life. Even as a very young child-priest, before he was cast out of the seminary, Will had begun to have his doubts. It seemed that God certainly moved in mysterious ways—most of them involving Will and his family members (*now deceased*, he thought)—in hand-to-hand combat with powerful Evil, personified in the ugliest bestial forms.

And some deceptively beautiful ones, he admitted, ruefully.

4

Who would have guessed that sweet-natured Kate, the young woman he'd fallen in love with, was actually a scheming, manipulative hussy—and, moreover, the murderously ambitious Jackie Nixon's daughter? And that despite their loving relationship, Kate had been playing him, all along?

Will had fallen in love with her. Fallen hard. And surely she had felt something for him…hadn't she? He had flashbacks of her expression as she gazed lovingly at him.

Had it all been a lie? He wasn't arrogant enough to believe it was impossible—unthinkable—that she had been duping him all along—that he was so irresistible to women!

But even in the hellish realms of the Darkness, even though she was a killer, he had discerned a softening of her eyes, a tenderness in her voice where he was concerned. He was sure their love had some basis in truth: that she had been touched by him, somewhere in her cold heart.

And now, as Victor Rothenstein had reported, Kate was pregnant…with Will's baby! And Jackie—his baby's grandmother and a newly 'turned' vampire who wanted to take over the world—intended to sacrifice the child for her evil ambitions! It was ridiculous, fantastical and far less realistic and believable than some of the plots of horror movies Will had laughed at, in his time.

It was all too hard for him to get his own head around, let alone tell anyone else. Imagine trying to explain all this to the police: *You have to let me out! I have to save my baby! A vampire queen is going to slaughter it for a ritual! I have to save the world!*

He had to trust that Victor had managed to stall them somehow. Or that the baby hadn't been born yet, and there was still time for him to get there. In her urgent greed for innocent blood, Jackie had used a growth-accelerating spell on the baby, still in Kate's womb. But Victor hadn't been able to tell Will how fast that would work.

With any luck, there was still time to save the baby. But what kind of baby would it be, born to a mother who had recently become a vampire? He had hardly had time to get his head around being a father, before he was told that the child was simply a pawn to be used in a game of death. With the baby's speed of development being artificially accelerated, by now it must be close to term. Meanwhile, Kate was in a spell-induced coma. The baby would receive no protection from either of its parents. No sooner would it take its first breath, then Jackie Nixon would sweep it away to slit its throat in a ritual ceremony to call forth the vampire legions.

Will cradled his head in his hands, his scalp prickling with sweat. It was all too much.

In the hours Will had spent in the police cell he'd had a great deal of time to think; filling his mind himself with whatever thoughts he could to block out Victor Rothenstein's attempts to speak to him through the telepathic connection the vampire had opened between them.

That was another laughable thing to explain to the police: *I know all these things because a three-thousand- year-old vampire is talking to me in my head! You have to believe me!*

6

Much as Will wondered what was happening outside these prison walls, it was too painful for him to bear Victor's insidious mind-whispering for long. For his own protection, he'd had to preserve his sanity and close himself off from the meditative process that made the connection secure and allowed them to talk, mind-to-mind.

For all Will knew, the child had been slaughtered already, and the legions of vampires were on the march, coming out from the Darkness where they had been slumbering for centuries, awaiting their release.

Evil the like of which had never been seen, was coming to Melas town. Or rather, coming *through* Melas—and the world was in danger.

But how do you begin to explain that to these bumpkins, the local police, whose only experience of crime was ticketing someone from out-of-town for running a red light?

However, Will knew that he was being flippant. Perhaps he should give the police force here more credit these days. After all, they'd had their own spate of murders in Melas, recently. Maybe the police weren't actually keen to pin it all on him.

He'd naturally kept quiet about the supernatural. He wasn't stupid! He was simply trusting that the facts would speak for themselves. He was innocent of Donovan Smith's murder, of course, but even in his defense, he couldn't tell the police about the vampires or anything else he knew about the terrible reality that faced them all. They'd just peg him as nuts. He'd had enough of incarceration just now, without giving them

7

cause to strap him in a straightjacket and cart him off to the local lunatic asylum.

Asylum...He rubbed his eyes with his fingertips, groaning gently. He had been just a boy when the old local asylum had been operational, and the forces of evil had first been unleashed around there. Only God knew what was happening now. While he was stuck there, in the police station, the *Grimoire Țepeș*—the ancient spell-book that had offered their only hope of preventing this evil from running to its full extent—was...where? He didn't even know where it was; nor in whose hands it lay.

Will knew he should have checked in with the vampire, Victor Rothenstein, to find out what was happening. But he dreaded doing so—especially while he was in police custody. He *had* felt Victor trying to get through: a gentle but painful tugging at his mind, like someone picking at the edges of a sore scab; but he'd resisted, since he knew that the pain and disgust he felt would greatly increase if Victor was allowed to communicate. It was all too physically, emotionally and mentally sickening to have that evil monster in his head for any length of time.

***

Beyond the interview room wall, Officer Lafitte was still explaining the situation to Cooley: "Besides, we got new information. The neighbor said she saw three people leaving the house shortly before the McConnellson boy arrived on the scene."

She went on, waving her sandwich at him: "A woman and two men. Eye witness swears to it. Plus, to top it all, this McConnellson fella used to be a priest! No previous. He's a fuckin' saint! And we just don't have sufficient evidence to keep him any longer—the only blood on him is a tiny trace, off that shreds of body parts where he fell on his side on the floor. And hell, that was nothing—only like he'd been lying on some cured bacon bits…"

Cooley swallowed, trying to forget that scene of horror, and the smell of cooked pork, but the flap of baloney dangling from the sandwich that Lafitte was waving didn't help matters at all.

She went on: "…And just a teeny touch of blood on one fingertip, where he said he dabbed it in a smeared footprint on the floor, to check what it was, when he first saw it…" She took another bite, then pushed the food to one side of her cheek like a chipmunk, to add in a voice muffled by food, "Not enough evidence to charge him. You and me had more blood on us than he did, by the time we'd walked through that room. CSI said they've never seen anything like it—no blood at all, hardly, amongst all that mess."

"Or—or—," Cooley snapped his fingers repeatedly. "Maybe—maybe it's like them other vampire killings! They drunk it all! That's why there's no blood!"

"Oh, for fuck's sake, Cooley," muttered Lafitte, picking some bread from between her teeth with a fingernail. "How many times I gotta tell you? There is no damn vampire killings!"

9

She wiped her hands down the sides of her uniform trousers and swung the interview door open. William sat upright in surprise.

Lafitte jerked her head towards the open hallway. "Okay," she said to the bewildered William. "You're good to go."

"For now," Cooley muttered, as William brushed past him, dazed.

***

William stood on the front step of the police station and breathed in the warm air. *It still doesn't taste like freedom*, he thought, tipping his face upwards and closing his eyes from the bright sun.

It seemed like a lifetime ago since his family had been killed and he'd come back to Melas again, embroiling himself in yet more fighting against Satanic powers. And things were only getting worse, not better. Somewhere out there, Will had an innocent baby of his own, as yet unborn, and in grave danger. If those evil bastards hadn't already killed it for their arcane ritual. But this time, it wasn't just personal.

The whole world is at stake! He opened his eyes, squinting at the suddenness of the bright sunlight.

Will stumbled down the step and into the road, not sure which direction to walk in. *Does it matter? Danger and evil is everywhere.* There was no escape, anyway. *Might as well meet it head-on.*

CHAPTER 2

Somewhere deep in the Darkness, something was stirring. Several things, in fact. Under the purple shadow of the ancient and imposing Vampire Castle with its thin, precariously balanced turrets, lay the vast and crumbling Vampire City. A desert of half-demolished buildings and dusty rubble, the abandoned city had stood empty since time immemorial, its vampire inhabitants asleep, spellbound, under an ancient curse.

However, the sleep-lock—which had kept the legions of vampires entombed in their coffins and crypts in a kind of suspended animation for centuries—had recently been lifted by the warlock Romeo Luiz's skillful magic, accompanied by Jackie Nixon's possession of the powerful spell book, the *Grimoire Țepeș*. Together, with an arcane ritual completed, they had succeeded in releasing the armies of the damned, without any need for an infant's blood. Now, slowly, the living dead were rising, one bony finger by one. One halting figure by one, they headed for the Vampire Castle.

Beneath the ruined buildings lay another sprawling city of subterranean crypts, their caskets containing the slumbering vampires. But now, they had been called to life again, and one by one, they responded. Stone and

11

lead coffin covers shifted gratingly aside; ancient preserved timber lids creaked slowly open; gray, bloodless fingers peeled themselves over the edges of tombs to gain balance and leverage, and the vampires rose stiffly, their limbs unused to movement, and made their steady way to the castle, to await instruction.

The gothic death-rock band, Belladonna Rose, was playing an impromptu concert in the castle's dismal grounds. Their music crashed around the eerie landscape, guitar patterns scything through the air, and the low-pitched bass line behind it all punctuated by Ash's hypnotic drumbeats. Rising occasionally above the music, came Bella's haunting voice, singing a dirge-like melody almost drowned by the clash of instruments. Behind them, the castle walls rose, hard and impenetrable—its arrow-slit eyes gazing suspiciously down on the assembled vampires below, and the band members, like black marionettes, jerking out their music, self-absorbed. Before them, the huge rusted iron gates hung lop-sided, their hinges decayed, so the heavy wrought iron barriers scraped the ground—opening out onto the desolate landscape that led to the deserted Vampire City, from whence came the slow march of individual vampires, heeding the call of their mistress.

Many of the vampires had assembled in the castle grounds, by now, and surrounded the band's makeshift stage area. But unlike Belladonna Rose's previous concert, in the grounds of Jackie Nixon's mansion—where the crowds of locals and partygoers had been loud, animated, active and full of life—this audience was largely still, silent, and full of death.

12

Regardless, the band played on. The music filtered its way through the arrow slits in the fortified walls and down the long corridors, into the castle chambers.

CHAPTER 3

Jackie Nixon was a powerful businesswoman in the earthly realm, but her powers in the hellish darkness were increasing with every undead soul that awakened. Jackie was now an all-powerful vampire leader—a self-defined Vampire Empress of all she surveyed. Moreover, once the legions were all arisen and prepared, she would take action outside and beyond the Darkness—and soon, she would rule over both the Darkness and the earth, too.

Next stop, heaven! she cackled to herself.

Jackie grinned into the silver mirror on the wall, her immaculately made-up face belying her years. After all, she was practically a grandmother! She shuddered. *No way!* She primped her hair, recently dyed a dark raven black again, running her scarlet fingernails through the glossy curtain cascading down over one side of her face, obscuring half of it. That would never do. She swept her hair back, clipping each side into a hair-slide, and then leant forward, admiring the well-defined structure of her cheekbones in the mirror. Then she stepped back to see herself full-length and smoothed her hands down over her hips, the blood-red velvet of her floor-length fitted gown warm to her touch.

She was aware of Romeo's lascivious gaze tracking down every curve of her body in the figure-hugging dress, but she ignored him and concentrated on her own image. She had been gratified to discover that it wasn't true that vampires had no reflections—or at least, they did have them, here: they still reflected in the Darkness. This was a very good thing, to Jackie's mind. Otherwise, how would she ever be able to tell how beautiful she was? And whether or not her make-up was applied correctly?

"Is it true, Romeo?" Jackie queried, dabbing the corner of her mouth with a white silk handkerchief. She wasn't sure if she had a spot of blood there from her last feed, or if it was a tiny bleed of red lipstick marring the fine outline around her collagen-plumped lips.

"Is *what* true, my Queen?" Romeo Luiz snaked a hand around her cinched waist, pulling her close to him. Both felt a frisson of sexual excitement, like an electrical charge between them.

"Is it true that vampirism keeps one younger?" She broke away from his embrace and admired herself again in the ornate mirror, with a smile of great approval, then turned around and looked hard at Romeo.

Romeo nodded, his mesmerizing eyes staring deeply into hers. "Darling, you are one of the Beautiful People. You will never grow old."

"I know that," she said, waving a dismissive, perfectly manicured hand. "But do I actually look younger, Romeo? I swear, I believe I do."

"Indeed," he said, humoring her. "Especially since the blood of virgins is particularly pure and youthful.

15

With every feed of maidens' blood, you are rejuvenated by their life-force."

"Pity there aren't more virgins around," Jackie said, bitterly.

Romeo threw back his head and laughed. "Every day, there are fewer, my dear. It is an impossible wish, to find a virtuous woman!"

"Sexist!" Jackie snapped, more instinctively from habit than with any real passion. Then, as if bored, she sighed and stepped back, leaning her weight on one foot, the other poised in front, thrusting one hip forward in a model's pose. She stood gazing mindlessly at the mirror, idly tapping a scarlet fingernail against her front tooth. Her thoughts had turned to her pregnant daughter in the next room, still sound asleep under a spell to prevent her from escaping with the precious baby.

"What is the matter, my Mistress?" Romeo asked.

"Hmmm…" Jackie hesitated, not knowing how much to tell Romeo. However, she needed his skills and knowledge, and as a relatively new vampire herself, she could not yet manage without him as a proficient warlock. Nor could she dispense with the ancient vampire, Victor Rothenstein, just yet. He was still incarcerated in a room down the corridor, chained by his neck to the wall. In fact, she had a number of loose ends to tidy up.

"I am still uncertain what to do with Kate, and her basta…the child," Jackie murmured, more to herself than to Romeo. "It's not as if I need the kid's blood, now that the sleep-lock is open, but…"

"I know, darling." Romeo stepped towards her and took her hand. "But as I told you, we can still use the

16

child for a blood sacrifice at a later stage—to increase your powers in the next phase of your development…" He pecked her cheek softly, and she could smell the ferrous tang of blood on his breath as he whispered in her ear: "And then, you will be unstoppable, my Queen!"

"But we don't really need the growth-spurt spell accelerating the pregnancy, now, do we?" Jackie said, thoughtfully.

Romeo pulled a face. "I guess not, since there is no longer such an urgency, now that the *Grimoire Ţepeş* and I have done our work. I guess you could even wake her up, for that matter."

Jackie gave him a sharp look. "Don't be ridiculous. I couldn't trust her not to run away!"

"She's your daughter." Romeo shrugged. "You know her best."

"Hmmm…" Jackie said doubtfully. "But—enough prevarication!" She swept around on the spot, the velvet skirt of her gown forming a swirling circle that arced widely around her ankles. "We have celebrations to attend!"

Romeo stepped closer again, smiling into her eyes, and resting his hands on her waist. "We have much to celebrate, Mistress!"

Her lips twitched, restraining a grin. "Indeed we have, Romeo."

"Then, if I may…" he gazed down at her bosom, and tentatively rested his fingertip on the front edge of the corset top of her gown, where her breast cleft appeared.

She raised one quizzical eyebrow—half amused; half daring him.

He picked at the thin cord bow that fastened the front of her corset, slowly drawing one end down, loosening the bow. "I suggest we rejoice in your victory."

"Hmmm?" she teased, not moving, not helping him.

"And maybe have our own private celebration?"

"Really?" she said drily, her lips pressed together to prevent a smile. "And what would that entail, exactly?"

He tugged the cord completely, so the bodice fell open, and her breasts tumbled out.

"This!" he hissed. Simultaneously, he bent forward and took one nipple in her mouth, suckling it whilst fondling the other breast with his warm hand.

Jackie groaned loudly and tossed back her head in ecstasy.

Romeo quickly scooped her up and threw her on the bed, rummaging up her long gown, while she urgently unzipped him, eager for him to plunge himself inside her.

And they rejoiced.

CHAPTER 4

Victor Rothenstein, the ancient vampire, sat on the floor with his back against the wall of the virtually empty castle chamber that held him prisoner. He was seething. Not only was he chained to the wall like a dog, constricted by a studded collar around his neck, but he was also frustrated that Will hadn't contacted him. For his part, Victor had consistently been trying to communicate with Will via the psychic communication channel he had set up the last time he saw him. And yet—no answer; no response.

Initially, Victor had wondered if Will was dead; but he didn't sense that. No. For whatever reason, Will was blocking him. Or being blocked, somehow. Had Jackie somehow cottoned on to their secret alliance? All Victor's senses were on the alert, looking for signs of her awareness.

He traced his mind for its memories of Jackie, the last couple of times he had seen her. Yes, he had tried to communicate with Will while she was in the same room. And yes, hadn't he seen her swing around suddenly, as if she had heard him speak? Or was he just being paranoid?

And yet here he was, unable to communicate with Will, after all. He brooded upon the point.

19

CHAPTER 5

Satiated by sex and success, Jackie and Romeo strolled through the shadowy grounds of the castle, careful to keep away from the crowds, so as not to be mobbed by either ancient vampires, or new vampires: the members of Belladonna Rose. They really need not have worried. Jackie and Romeo were flanked by two demon guards, seven feet tall, with scaly reptilian skin, long tails, and claws—who were deterrent enough for the fiercest adversary, let alone the obsequious vampires who only wished to do Jackie's bidding. The ancient vampires were docile and respectful, and the band were still playing—the music much louder here, outside the thick castle walls.

"Let's go to the cave," Jackie murmured lazily, still lethargic from the energetic sex they had enjoyed less than an hour before. A short post-coital nap had done nothing to renew her energies.

Romeo stopped in surprise. "The cave? Why? There should be nothing to see!"

"Exactly," said Jackie, tugging on his hand, urging him forward. "I want to make sure of that."

They wandered out of the public's view, through the massive, dilapidated gates, and around the wall, towards the cliff at the back of the castle that stood above the dark, rocky beach. Jackie had grown used to the purple glow of the castle, almost forgetting how black the Darkness was, although her eyes had acclimatized during their walk, and the purple luminescence still shed some reflected light on the sea, like moonlight.

The sluggish, gray sea rolled in gelatinously, making barely a sound. Still, above the high, thick walls of the castle grounds, they could hear the distant noise of Belladonna Rose's music, muffled by thick stone walls and yards and yards of space between the two silent mystical figures and the far-away raucous band.

At the top of the cliff edge, Romeo stopped dead, and said, "There."

Looking down, their eyes picked out glints of jagged rock, and then Jackie saw a block of cavernous darkness—a large, dark, flat boulder that was huge, easily the size of her mansion, and of an impenetrable blackness that appeared to reflect no light: just a massive black plate of inscrutable depth.

"But there's nothing to see," whispered Jackie, feeling unaccountably in awe.

"You should be glad about that," Romeo answered, pulling her closer.

She shivered, even though the air was warm. "And the Red Beast of Hell really slumbers, there?"

"Let us hope it is still slumbering!"

Jackie peered down, squinting her eyes, trying to make out anything more—any details of the dimensions of the massive stone that blocked the cave, or any distinguishing features of what might lie therein.

21

"It seems…" she murmured, "…such an innocuous place. Such a relatively small prison for such a fearsome, all-powerful entity."

"That is just the stopper to the bottle that lets the genie out," Romeo said, gently rubbing her shoulders, as if he instinctively felt her internal chill.

"And then, after you release the stopper, all hell breaks loose."

"Literally," Romeo agreed, and kissed the top of her head.

She was aware that she felt small and helpless, like a child. "Shouldn't there be…I don't know…smoke coming out, or something?" she asked, staring into the darkness. Nothing. All was still.

Romeo shrugged. "I suppose we should be worried if there was smoke or something. Wouldn't that mean there was a leak, somewhere? That the seal wasn't secure?"

"I guess so," she conceded. Still feeling oddly vulnerable—not an emotion she recognized as familiar—she huddled further in the cave of Romeo's arms, and asked: "And the Red Beast definitely can't get out of there?"

Romeo chuckled. "Not unless we release it."

CHAPTER 6

The door to the chamber in which Victor lay prisoner was flung wide open on its hinges by one of the demon guards, the sound of it hitting the wall behind it with a crash jerking Victor out of his uneasy slumber.

"I said 'open the door', not 'kick the door in'!" boomed Jackie Nixon's voice. "Fool!"

The tall, gray scaly figure bent his head beneath the doorframe to enter the space, then held open the door, and bowed, with a flourish.

Jackie Nixon, Vampire Queen, swept in, in all her resplendent glory; the rich, scarlet velvet skirt of the gown rippling in her wake, and taking a couple of seconds to settle as she stood still, across the room. Victor observed that the hem of her floor-length gown was muddy and stained with water. She had evidently been outside the castle gates.

Just to test his theory, Victor watched Jackie's expression carefully as he tried contacting Will through telepathy, saying in his mind, *Will! Will, are you there?*

To Victor's surprise and horror, after all this time, Will actually answered, "Yes! Yes, I am!"

Jackie's eyes widened slightly, then narrowed as she stared at Victor. That was enough of a sign for him. She

23

walked slowly and determinedly across the room towards him, hips swaying.

I was right! he thought.

"Right about what?" Will asked, telepathically.

With a shock, Victor realized that he would have to be careful of his thoughts, and differentiate them from his communication with Will, since Jackie could obviously hear everything he was saying.

All is well, here! he lied, for her benefit.

Will started talking, hurriedly, "Victor, I need to know, is the baby—?"

Alive and well, Victor interrupted. *Everything is fine.*

Afraid of what Will might say next, Victor quickly shut down the psychic channel between them.

With a frown, Jackie stood waiting, evidently for more.

Can I run interference? Victor wondered. Having closed off from Will, he wondered if he could lead Jackie to believe he was still in contact with him, and say something that might buy him time. Misguide her. He thought fast.

"When are you going to let me go?" Victor gasped.

Jackie Nixon threw back her head and laughed. "Oh, Victor! You really think I am going to just let you go? Especially when you..." here she leant down, and snarled, in his face, "are a deceitful, lying traitor!"

24

CHAPTER 7

William's car was still parked where he had left it, in the center of Melas, on the new development that Donovan Smith's company had been building. He sat inside it, the key in the ignition but the engine not yet started, thinking deeply. He couldn't connect with Victor any more. After spending so long staving off Victor's thoughts from entering his head, after he had blocked Victor's every attempt—now Victor's connection was lost? What did that mean?

Victor said everything was fine. But still, Will had his doubts.

Frankly, he was relieved that Victor's contact had been so short. Will knew that he needed to talk to Victor Rothenstein at length, soon. He had blocked him for so long, it had been a strain on his resources. But he still couldn't face it.

And yet, it was odd. Should he believe that the baby was still alive? That all was well?

Obviously, the world hadn't ended. Yet.

Victor's words had spoken deeply to an integral part of Will that yearned for things to be fine. He truly wanted to believe that. He wanted to wake up and find that it had all been a dream. A nightmare—all in his head—and now he was awake again, everything was okay.

The sun has got its hat on! Nope. He'd thought that 'aloud'. No response from Victor. For the first time in a number of days, Will couldn't feel the burden of Victor's simmering evil weighing on his mind. For the first time in a long time, Will felt free. *Hip-hip-hip-hooray!*

He started the car engine, and a smile stretched his face. It felt unfamiliar to him—using muscles he was unaccustomed to employing.

Up to this point, there had been a cost to keeping Victor out of his mind. But now, Will felt in a holiday mood. While he had been held in the police station, Will's head had been too full of pain and exhaustion to enable him to open himself up to Rothenstein's thoughts through the psychic connection. And besides, while Will had been in police custody, in danger of being prosecuted for a heinous murder, he'd needed his wits about him. He still did. There was much to do.

But before that, he felt the need for some respite—and some support. He'd already thought about the only person alive who could offer him that.

He pulled the handbrake off, eased the car off the Melas development, and began to drive in the direction of Cleveland, Ohio.

CHAPTER 8

Victor lay on the floor, feeling beaten in mind, body and spirit. He hadn't even had time to consider a plan, or a way of using the fact to his advantage that Jackie could evidently hear vampire-communicated thoughts with humans. At least, she evidently could, with humans who had been ritually introduced to the system of telepathy. The violence had been too sudden and immediate for Victor to use any of his wiles.

One of the demon guards had kicked him repeatedly, after he'd first been punched almost senseless by the other guard, on Jackie's orders. *A stake through the heart would have been a blessing,* he'd thought, as the demonic attack continued.

"Why don't you just kill me?" he asked, while he still had breath.

"For one reason," Jackie said, holding up one scarlet-varnished talon, "I like to see you suffer. And two…" Another scarlet flash of fingernail joined the first. "I might still need you." She leant in towards his bruised and bloodied face. "Yes!" She nodded rapidly, eyes wide. "I know! I don't like it, either! But there, we have it. I might still need you because you are the oldest vampire I know, with the most knowledge, who has recently been living between the two worlds. You still

27

have some value. Unfortunately." She stood upright and sashayed away. "Don't think this arrangement doesn't disappoint me as much as it disappoints you."

The heavy door closed behind her, and Victor rested his face back down on the hard floorboards, in a pool of his own blood. His vision blurring, he closed his eyes involuntarily and submitted to blessed unconsciousness at last.

***

It had been hours since Victor had contacted Will, and Will's initial relief had given way to concern. He tried to push that out of his mind while he drove to Cleveland, turning up the music when worries threatened to pervade his mind—singing loudly to keep the words of doubt from filling his head. He kept reassuring himself: Victor had said everything was okay, the baby was safe—which meant that the sleep-lock was still secure. The vampires must still be asleep—mankind was not at risk, the sun was still shining—and the earth was still spinning. All was right with the world at least as far as Will could tell. He had a niggling feeling that wasn't true, but for now, he chose to convince himself, since he desperately needed some R&R. As he stood on the front step of Natasha Thayer's house, knocking at the door, he hoped he would receive some.

The door was cautiously opened, and the tiny frame of Natasha Thayer filled the crack in the doorway. Upon seeing Will, her hazel eyes opened wide in surprise.

"Will?"

He smiled sheepishly, aware that he had rudely hurried away after their last lovemaking, with barely a goodbye, hot on the trail of the *Grimoire Țepeș* as soon as he'd had a hint of where it was. He held out his hands, shrugged, and gave her an apologetic look. "So sorry I had to leave so fast, last time, Natasha!"

"Hmmm," she said, leaning against the doorframe, arms folded, with an expression of sternness on her face. Her dark hair was scraped back into a high ponytail, and for all that she was nearly twice Will's age—in her late thirties—even without makeup, she looked pretty, young and hot. Although at that moment, she also looked angry. She tapped one foot in irritation, although the flat rubber-soled pumps she was wearing made no sound.

"I had to go…" Will reiterated, his face reddening. Under his collar, he felt his skin steam with embarrassment and uncertainty. "As you know…. it was a matter of urgency!"

She raised one eyebrow, still looking angry. Then burst out laughing. "Hahaha! Hooo! I couldn't keep up the act!" She threw her arms around him, and he smelt vanilla and coconut in her hair.

"Pee-yoo!" she pulled away and held him at arm's length, her nose wrinkling in disgust. "What the hell? You smell like you've been sleeping in a pig-sty!"

"Close enough," Will admitted. "I've been in a police cell a couple of days…"

"What the hell, Will?" she repeated, and saw his mouth opening to explain, but she tugged him by the hem of his grubby white T-shirt, pulling him inside the house. "Never mind—explain in a moment. Of course, I'm pleased to see you. But they didn't let you shower?" Natasha said, her voice high-pitched in wonder. "Isn't that a basic human right? Well, you come right up, into the bathroom with me!"

She closed the front door behind him, ushering him towards the stairs. "First of all, did you get the *Grimoire Țepeș?*"

"No," Will admitted.

"Oh, Wi-ill!" she squeaked in mock-horror. "You mean, you left me standing alone, bereft and lonely, all in a post-coital haze, for nothing?"

She pushed him upstairs, while he gabbled his most recent story and explanation, telling her everything.

As she ran the shower for him, and he peeled off his sweat-stained clothes, she listened in horror. "Jeez, Will. I'm sorry I joked. I mean…My goodness! You're lucky to be alive!"

"So, I don't even know what's going on, anymore," he said, side-stepping her to get into the shower cubicle.

She smelt the strong musky scent of his skin, but her senses were more taken by his taut muscular body, the breadth of his shoulders, and the definition of his abdominal muscles as he turned under the spray of the shower. And her eyes strayed down to his tempting cock and balls. She felt a quiver inside her, deep within her inner labia, and she stepped fully clothed into the cubicle with him.

"Wha…?" he laughed, as the water streamed down her face, and her wet blouse clung tightly to her breasts, accentuating her hard nipples beneath. Will stood stock still, bewildered.

"We need to do something life-affirming," she smiled, eyes closed against the splashes of water that streamed down onto them both. On her tip-toes, she reached her face up towards him, while he leant down, and they kissed, long and deep. Then she broke away as suddenly as she'd started kissing him. She took the soap from his useless hands, a mischievous grin on her face, and rubbed the bar until it was frothing between her own hands in a thick lather.

"You're very...dirty," she breathed into his face, dropping the soap.

His eyes widened in surprise to feel her grab his cock in one of her small hands, cupping his balls in the other, and she started rubbing the slippery lather up and down the thick shaft of his penis. He groaned, lost.

"Just thought I'd..." she leant closer against him, her fingers sliding faster, firmly up and down. "...give you a hand."

He reached down and fumbled urgently with the waistband of her wet trousers, swiftly pulling them down her thighs, and pushing his fingers between her legs, as she shimmied out of her drenched pants. She moaned, tipping her pubic mound towards him, eagerly, and hooking one leg around him.

He had felt dead—completely dead up to now—and she was right. He needed to feel alive! Her tiny hands, slick with soap and water, worked quicker, and he throbbed, hot...It was impossible...he was afraid...afraid...couldn't bear it! He gently pushed her fingers away with one hand, then placed his arms around her back and cupped the cheeks of her buttocks, one in each hand, lifting her up onto his erection with a full-

31

throated grunt as she slid down, taking him all in, with a shudder. She gave a small cry and curled her legs around his hips, where they fitted perfectly.

CHAPTER 9

"Who the hell is that?" drawled Jackie Nixon, lifting up one side of her eye mask, on hearing the distant sound of the doorbell.

She was lounging full-length on the leather couch in her drawing room, back at her earthly home in the Madison House in Melas. It was so much more comfortable than the dark, cold castle, and she loved her luxuries. Besides, she still had work to do in the earth realm, despite the slow assembly of vampires in the Darkness below the house.

One such thing she needed was a nap. She needed to recoup her energy, and as for naps, the couch was better...lying in a coffin in some cobweb-covered crypt was not her thing.

The blinds of the house were down, as they always were during the daytime, even though it was not yet dusk: to protect its vampire mistress from the fatal daylight that could do her irreparable damage if she allowed it to come anywhere near her. She had no intention of crumbling, screeching, into a pile of dust like some sixpenny Nosferatu from an old horror movie. Therefore, she'd had her new home entirely adapted to filter out all light, with particularly effective tinted glass in the windows and heavy, impenetrable blinds and drapes utilized most of the time. It was a veritable fortress against sunlight.

The maid opened the heavy drawing room door. "Madam, it's the police…"

Jackie cursed under her breath and sat upright, ripping off her eye-mask in irritation.

"Two detectives, Madam."

Jackie got up, growling to herself and straightening her clothes. "I suppose you'll have to show them in."

"Madam." The woman gave a deferential nod, and retreated; her footsteps clip-clopped down the hallway, where she had left the two men standing awkwardly. She returned seconds later, by which time Jackie had already poured herself a Scotch. Jackie had reckoned she might need it.

"Detective Bottles and Detective Vincent, Madam," the maid announced.

"Yes, yes," Jackie said airily, waving her crystal glass so that the generous Scotch and soda sloshed over the side.

Gary Bottles and Rich Vincent strode in—all serious business.

"What can I do for you, gentlemen?" Jackie asked tightly.

"Good day, Ma'am," said Gary Bottles, determined to observe the social niceties, even if the lady of the house didn't.

He was a lean, blond man, dressed in a smart gray suit, with an open-necked shirt, although Jackie wished he'd gone the whole hog and worn a tie. His throat looked just a little too tempting. She watched his Adam's apple bob as he spoke in an attempt to distract

34

herself from the prominent vein at the side of his neck. She could almost hear the blood pulsing through it.

"We're from the Harrison County Sheriff's Department. We're investigating the disappearance of a young man—a Bobby Arlen?" he went on.

Jackie pulled a face. "Never heard of him."

Rich Vincent, a more muscular man than his associate, had been standing with his hands on his hips, a slight paunch straining the front of his polo-shirt beneath his dark blue blazer. Jackie noticed that his polo-shirt was tucked into his light tan chinos. She hated that. *Either wear a damn dress shirt, or wear a t-shirt loose, like God meant you to!*

Rich Vincent had been listening whilst surveying the room up to this point, taking in the expensive décor and wondering about the blinds darkening the room, as well as the artificial glow of the table lamps employed, even though it was still daylight outside.

Now, he stepped forward and presented a photo to Jackie with the same directness as he presented his police shield to citizens. In one deft movement, he could whip his police credentials out of his inside pocket and flash it up in front of someone's eyes within one second flat. His partner, Gary, called it 'the ole' whip'n'flash'' Rich's wife once said it was '*As if you're fending off a vampire with a crucifix!*'

Here, he turned his acute gaze on Jackie and employed the same technique on her, holding Bobby Arlen's image at arm's length in front of her face. "Recognize him?"

35

"Oh, I don't think so," Jackie said, giving a cursory glance to the photo, then looking away, as if bored already. She sipped her drink nonchalantly.

In reality, the face of the young man triggered something in her memory. *It's that kid who came along as Lex's sister's date,* she recalled, although she said nothing aloud to the detectives. The sight of the young man's face evoked a particular flashback, since she remembered watching the pair arguing over something that night. It was the fact that it was Lex's sister he'd been with that had stuck in her memory—and it was a birthday party in Lex's honor, after all; otherwise, Jackie would have had no idea who the hell the kid was. In all likelihood, Lex or one of the others had simply killed him. There were so many that night—how was she meant to remember them all? Their blood had spilled onto the floors of the house, which drank it in, greedily; their corpses were absorbed into the very atoms of the house's structure within minutes. No one would find a trace of them now, so Jackie felt she had nothing to fear. Especially not from these small-town cops. Especially not now, when she was on the brink of something earth-shattering—apocalyptic, in fact. The souls of those sacrificed here in the Madison House had enabled Jackie's power to increase in magnitude. They had all added to the intense force that had eventually opened the sleep-lock, releasing the vampire legions who awaited her command now, back in the Darkness.

"We've had a report that he attended a party here, recently," Rich Vincent went on, eyeing her vagueness with suspicion.

36

"I don't recall…I must say. Which party?" she asked, mildly.

Gary Bottles cleared his throat, reading from a tiny notebook in his hand. His blond fringe flopped down over his lowered eyes, as he peered down at the small print. "A *birthday* party, ma'am. For an…Alexander Wilderstein—known as 'Lex Wilde'—of the band Belladonna Rose?"

"Oh, Lex? Yes. My house was hired for the event. I must say, I don't really know him, myself."

"And he's now missing."

"Oh, dear." Jackie shrugged, as if to say, 'What can you do?' and took a large swig of Scotch and soda.

"Where you here yourself on that night, Ma'am?" Bottles asked politely.

"I was, for part of the evening, detective," Jackie answered, walking towards him, flashing him a disarming smile. His skin was so pale she could see the veins through its transparency, and she was entranced by it. "But then, you know, I largely left them to it. After all—they were just young people—kids, really, and I am…" She fixed him with an intense gaze, and added huskily, "…I'm rather more mature…Wouldn't you say, detective?"

Gary Bottles coughed, his face brightening red. "Oh. No, Ma'am." He cleared his throat again, nervously. "What time would you say you were actually here at the party…approximately?"

Jackie's voice tinkled with laughter. "Goodness! I can't recall. It must have been…Well, of course, I was here early evening onwards until…just after midnight. Then, I went to…" She leant close in towards Bottles, her breath warm on his face. "...bed, detective. I need my beauty sleep. Don't you think?"

Gary Bottles swallowed hard, trying to recover his composure. "No, Ma'am."

Rich Vincent observed the exchange, feeling detached, simply scientifically watching the tics and tells of the others from a distance, as if analyzing the effects of doctored bait on a couple of lab rats. It was a technique he used often, and one he wished that Gary would learn. Rich was forever having to overcompensate for his partner's occasional flummoxed thinking and flustered behavior whenever he encountered beautiful women. And here it was—again.

Rich knew Jackie Nixon only by reputation: powerful businesswoman, investor and savior of Melas. And yes, still attractive for a middle-aged woman, probably in her fifties, but wealthy enough to have had plenty of cosmetic work done to retain her youth. But Rich Vincent's sixth-sense told him that she was a real piece of work. Hell, no—what was he talking about? *All* of his senses told him that. He coolly observed her moves on his partner—the blatant flirting, like a close-up magician using sleight of hand to get one over on the bewildered punter. *The woman is brazen!* part of him yelled. But there just wasn't anything Rich could put his finger on—no proof, no evidence that she had anything to do with the disappearance of powerful Senator John Arlen's twenty-year-old only son.

It wasn't like this was a street-kid, or a hobo, or just some drug-addicted runaway—one of those vulnerable kids from a chaotic background, voted 'most likely to end up in a body-bag' in his high-school yearbook. No, this kid was seriously privileged and destined for greatness.

Fuckin' Princeton boy! even Gary had exclaimed. *Senator's son! Jeez! Our balls are gonna be on the line, here!*

Whatever happened, the Senator would not be letting this lie.

"Please...think...carefully," Gary was advising Jackie Nixon, enunciating his words slowly. "Did...you...see...this young man...at that party? Or...anywhere?"

"No...I...did...NOT!" Jackie mimicked, her face straight, although Rich thought he saw amusement dancing behind her eyes. And he didn't like that, one bit.

Gary sighed, turned his face towards Rich, out of Jackie's view, and grimaced helplessly.

Rich stepped forward. "We are going to need a list of guests who attended the party, if you please, Mrs Nixon."

"I would absolutely love to help you, detective...s." She looked to each of them in turn, beaming a smile. "But as I said, it wasn't my party. You would have to speak to Lex Wilde about that, I'm afraid."

"Don't worry," Rich said stiffly. "We will. Thank you for your help, Mrs Nixon." He gave Gary a stiff nod, and they both made to leave.

"Oh," Jackie placed a hand on Gary's chest, stopping him in his tracks. "Before you go, both of you—are you anywhere nearer to finding out who killed Donovan Smith?"

Gary looked down at her hand, where it remained on his chest, and gulped.

39

"I'm afraid we're not at liberty…" Rich commenced, only to be interrupted immediately.

"He was, after all, a close personal friend of myself…and my…extremely powerful husband, sadly deceased." She looked meaningfully into Gary's eyes. "You *do* know who I am, detective?"

"We initially arrested some psycho kid –William McConnellson III—" Gary gabbled.

"We can't discuss ongoing investigations, Ma'am," Rich said loudly, interrupting Gary's urgent muttering.

Gary opened his eyes wide, Jackie's hand still flat against his heart, and his mouth continued to run off, as if in spite of himself: "But we let him go because we had no evidence. He couldn't have committed the crime. And now he seems to have skipped town."

"Come on!" growled Rich, incredulously.

"Is that all?" Jackie asked, staring into Gary's eyes, her scarlet-varnished fingernails still splayed across his chest.

"Yes," he coughed, and after another second of staring hard at him, she removed her hand. He reeled back on his heels, one hand pressed to his chest where her hand had been a moment before. He stumbled after his partner, who was already on his way out of the door, walking briskly down the hallway, his limbs stiff with anger. Gary Bottles had to run to catch him up.

"What the hell, Bottles?" Rich whispered between gritted teeth once his partner was next to him, still marching towards the front door. He was seething. "What—she give you some kind of truth drug? What?"

"I…I don't know…" Gary stammered, confused, as they made their way out of the house.

Back in the drawing room, Jackie stared into space, her hand distractedly placing her Scotch glass on a side table without any awareness.

So, she mused, *it seems that William McConnellson III is out and about.*

CHAPTER 10

In the half-moonlight that filtered through the open bedroom window into Herman Thayer's old house, Will lay staring up at the ceiling, thinking deeply, while Natasha, Herman's niece, slept soundly next to him. Both of them had been exhausted by their frenzied lovemaking. Will had tried his best to be loving afterwards, as they talked awhile, his arms around her petite form—since he knew that women liked that kind of thing—but to his chagrin, he had quickly fallen unconscious. After driving for hours, all his remaining energy had gone into sex, and he had nothing left to give, emotionally or otherwise. So, at some point, he had simply lost consciousness completely.

Now, hours later, he had woken up feeling refreshed, only to see that it was the middle of the night and Natasha had evidently rolled over long ago and was happily fast asleep, breathing deeply and heavily.

So, left to his own devices, with his mind alert, he was free to consider all that had gone on, and try to come to a conclusion on what to do next. And eventually, he decided, it was time. He swallowed hard, his heart thumping in his chest. He closed his eyes, steadied his breathing, and allowed his mind to relax before he reached out with his thoughts.

42

Victor? He paused, holding his breath in anticipation as he waited. He tried again: *Victor...Are you there?*

His mind became aware of an insidiously evil presence, seeping slowly into his own psyche, and he shuddered.

"Of course I'm here," came Victor's voice. "Where the hell have you been? Where are you?"

Cleveland, Will answered.

"Cleveland*? Fucking* Cleveland?"

Ohio, Will clarified.

"I know where Cleveland is!" Victor snapped. "But why?"

Will physically shrugged, even though he knew Victor couldn't see him. He had no explicable answer for Victor. An image of Natasha came into his head: smiling, her freckled nose wrinkling in delight to see him. How could he possibly explain, when he had no rational answer, himself? *For company? To feel loved? To feel alive?*

"Oh, well, ex-CUSE me, if I don't make you feel loved and alive!" Victor scoffed, his tone dripping in sarcasm, and Will's face burnt red as he realized that Victor had heard his own thoughts, not just the words that he intentionally spoke to Victor in his head. He recognized that he would have to be careful.

What's the matter? Will asked him.

"What the fuck?" Victor exclaimed. "You went off, on vacation?"

You said everything was cool.

"I had to tell you that, because Jackie Nixon was listening. Everything, in fact, is most uncool. The sleep-lock is opened..."

The baby? cried Will, sitting bolt upright. *She killed it?*

"No! She didn't need the fucking baby! She has the Grimoire, and Romeo Luiz, whose power as a warlock I underestimated..." Victor snarled. "They opened the sleep-lock, anyway, and the vampires are assembling..."

Holy shit! said Will. How could he not know this already? He couldn't understand how this apocalyptic event was occurring, yet all seemed to be fine in the world. *But.. but...what's happening? I can't see any sign of anything, here...*

"Oh, yeah, everything's great in OHIO!" Victor snapped. "As yet, the vampire legions are still not fully empowered—they are more like zombies—unthinking, passive. Only when all of them arise from their caskets and are commanded by their ruler will they receive complete rejuvenation. And so, they are still awaiting instruction. But it's only a matter of time."

What? What can we do? Will leapt out of bed, scanning the dimly illuminated room, looking for his clothes. Then he remembered that Natasha had flung them all in the washer, since he had been wearing them for days. *Fuck! Fuck!* He tore open the door of Herman Thayer's old walnut wardrobe, fingered through the tweed suits and grabbed a shirt.

"What can we do?" Will said aloud. Natasha turned over in bed, with a groan.

Victor's voice permeated Will's panic: "As it is, our only hope now—before the newly-awakened vampires fully regain their strength—is for you to return to Melas and destroy the Madison House."

44

Me? Will said, breaking into more of a sweat, his fingers fumbling, buttoning up the shirt. *Isn't there anything you can do, over there? I'm miles away from Melas—and you're still in the Darkness, I presume?*

Victor seethed. "Don't you think I would do something, if I could? She still has me chained up here like a dog, and I can't use my powers in these circumstances."

Victor's face was set with fury, had Will only been able to see it. It rankled the vampire greatly that he was worse than a slave to Jackie Nixon. Once he was free, his vengeance would know no bounds. His very being vibrated with the powerful desire to assume the position that should rightfully be his, before this ingénue usurper, this megalomaniac, Jackie Nixon, had come on the scene. Victor was the oldest, most powerful vampire, after all! That he should be reduced to this recently-human's lackey was unthinkable! Victor was furious. Oh! When Victor was out of her power, would she get what was coming to her! And this boy—Will—would be dispensable once Victor had used him to achieve his freedom and stop Jackie Nixon in her tracks. Until then, Victor had to pretend they were allies, which they were, to the degree that they had to stop Jackie in her tracks. After that, for Victor, it was open season on human ex-priest-boys.

So it's all down to me, then? Will said, psychically.

"I will do what I can," Victor growled. "But until you get me out of these shackles and from under Jackie Nixon's spell, all I can do is give you information and advice."

"Fuck!" Will exclaimed aloud. Natasha gave a louder groan and lifted herself up on one elbow, scratching her head, her hair forming a ruffled curtain over her face.

So all you are is...some call-handler for emergency services? Will transmitted to Victor. *Like...you can only talk me through it?*

"Except nobody else is coming to your aid at all," Victor warned. "It's all down to you. You have to deal with the biggest emergency the universe has ever faced."

"What are you doing?" Natasha's voice was thick with sleep.

"Saving the world," said Will, aloud.

***

Having finished communicating with Will, Victor gingerly eased himself into a sitting position on the floor with a sharp intake of breath and inch by inch, settled back down with his back against the wall. *Ouch!* Every part of his body ached from the rough beating he had recently received. *Damn!* No vampire should be treated like this—unable to use most of his powers and denied his superhuman strength, even to defend himself. The studded dog-collar he was forced by Jackie Nixon to wear around his neck weakened him to an unimaginable degree and—in addition to its practical purpose—there was the factor of his degradation and the humiliation he was suffering in wearing a dog-collar and being chained to a ring in the wall.

46

She should be bowing down before ME! he raged. His face twisted into a grimace of disgust, and he winced, touching his swollen lip. He had been tasting his own blood for hours and his mouth still hurt where the demon guards had kicked and punched him. Tentatively, Victor pinched his thumb and forefinger around his right upper fang, and wobbled it from side to side, holding his breath. Fortunately, it wasn't loose at all. He sighed with relief. A vampire, if de-fanged, would die, since he couldn't feed adequately. Or else, he would be dependent on others to bring him prey, and to facilitate the bloodletting for him, like a geriatric human in a nursing home, being spoon-fed mush. Another humiliation. Another thing that would have made him vulnerable.

Still, he had escaped that fate more by luck than by design. Had Jackie Nixon known this fact about defanging, or thought about the implications—for all he knew—she would have instructed the guards to de-fang him on purpose.

Victor fumed at the thought of his powerlessness. His frustration was almost palpable, hanging in the atmosphere, surrounding him in the barren room—its cloying stench making him nauseous. But he knew he had to pull himself around to maintain the strength of mind to put his plan into action now that the time had come. And Will was still central to his strategy to overthrow Jackie Nixon, and take over the mantle as ruler of the vampire legions. After that—the world!

Victor shook his bruised head. *Mustn't get ahead of myself!*

47

Once Jackie realized that the vampires couldn't leave the Darkness without Victor's key personal input, Victor knew that she would be forced to bargain with him. He smiled at the thought, and jumped in pain again, as his bloodied skin stretched tightly around his grin.

She will soon find out that she needs me more than she knows. She will be forced to agree to share power with me, in ruling over the vampire kingdom, he told himself, warming at the thought. *And later, in ruling over the human world.* He rubbed his hands together with pleasure, adding: *If she lasts that long.*

CHAPTER 11

Their features hazy in the purple gloom of the foreground just below the castle walls, a sea of individual vampires extended invisibly in all directions, far into the profound black of the Darkness. Their ragged clothing was dusty from centuries of lying in their cold stone crypts or decaying wooden caskets, and they stood silently surrounding the Vampire Castle in the purple glow of the realm. Waiting.

"Why don't I send them out now?"

Bringing Romeo Luiz with her, Jackie had fled back to the Darkness upon hearing the news that the police had let William McConnellson free. She stood with her hands on the mullioned window frame set into the cold castle wall, gazing out on the immobile army of vampires as far as the eye could see beyond the eerie light emanating from the purple-glowing castle. It was impossible to see how far they reached into the black of the Darkness itself.

"With that defrocked boy-priest out on the loose," she snarled, "we need to act fast. The vampire army is assembled, more or less—no?"

"It might be wiser to wait...um...until all of them are here...and then they will probably be more collectively conscious of your commands," Romeo said,

49

his voice betraying his hesitancy to advise on such points.

Jackie spun around, fixing him with a stare. "What do mean, 'it might be'—'probably'? Don't you know what you're talking about?"

Romeo grimaced, his handsome features twisting into ugly uncertainty, which told Jackie all she needed to know.

She roared, "I need assurance! I need knowledge! You are supposed to be a powerful warlock. Have you been bullshitting me all along?"

"By no means!" Romeo exclaimed, outraged. He puffed out his chest with indignation. "I have given you the best advice and guidance as far as my knowledge of magic and spell-casting is concerned! This is simply outside my area of expertise. And after all, this event is unprecedented. I can only give my thoughts and guesses on such matters—since I do not have the specialist experience, nor the facts. Victor Rothenstein is your vampire expert!"

Jackie Nixon cursed under her breath. She hated having to rely on other people—most of all, Victor Rothenstein—for things that were outside her control. The sooner she held power over all these creatures in both realms, the better. She was especially reluctant to go crawling to Victor Rothenstein asking for favors just now, after having him beaten unconscious by her demon guards. Was she not already Queen of the Vampires, in effect? If she were to be an all-powerful entity, she must do without the likes of the pathetic traitor, Rothenstein, to decide her next steps.

50

Simmering with anger through gritted teeth, Jackie growled, "From your 'thoughts and guesses', then, what would happen if I commanded the vampire legions to do my bidding, right now? To leave the darkness and wreak havoc on the earth? Now."

Romeo shrugged. "I imagine they will do so, although without their full collective power."

"Hmmm." Jackie went over to the window again, and surveyed the dismal troops, standing mindlessly awaiting instruction. There looked to be a great many there, already. All awaiting her command.

Surely there are enough here, and there are still more—those without number in the black of the Darkness—where no eyes can see them? There must be thousands, if not millions. Standing. Waiting. Doing nothing without my authority.

"Then, let's do it," she said, definitely. "Now."

Romeo Luiz swallowed down his doubt and gave a small bow of the head in assent. "As you wish."

"So, how do I set about it?" she said, staring intently at his face, as if to scrutinize every possible behavioral tic and blink of his eyes for signs of weakness or ignorance. "I presume some kind of ritual or something?"

"No," Romeo answered confidently. "The ritual opening of the sleep-lock has sufficed. They naturally obey the opener."

"Not you!?" She pursed her lips hard, scowling. "You were the warlock whose magic opened it!" Her eyes blazed.

"No!" Romeo answered quickly. "Of course not. You, my queen. They obey only you. Since they would

51

otherwise still be slumbering, the vampires obey the person who powerfully commanded and authorized the ritual opening. Not the mere servant who fulfilled her command."

"Then tell me, what do I do now, to send them into the earth realm, en masse?" she asked. "I warn you: my patience is growing thin, warlock."

Romeo knew that he had to respond with authority himself, since she was in no mood for prevarication. "Simply command them, aloud, with true intent and laser-like focus," he answered.

Before he had even finished the sentence, Jackie Nixon had swept out of the door in a swirl of red velvet skirt, leaving Romeo standing by himself in the empty room.

He hurried after her, well aware of the stiff, determined set of her shoulders as she strode out of the external door and onto the broad stone balcony overlooking the courtyard immediately beneath the castle. As they had done for the past several days, numerous vampires stood below, huddled together in their dusty hordes, a ragged, broken rag-tag army. They weren't the kind of forces that made Jackie proud to command them. This all looked very inauspicious to Jackie Nixon, and she tasted the bitterness of doubt.

When she appeared on the balcony and rested her hands on the stone parapet, as if as one, all of the vampires raised their gray faces towards her like eerie color-drained sunflowers turning towards the sun. Looking down on them, Jackie recognized for the first time that, like humans, each one was an individual with unique features. She had otherwise just seen them as an amorphous mass—a crowd without singular members. Some were young children; some beautiful teenagers; many of them adults in the strong prime of their 'afterlife'. And then, there was something else that shocked Jackie: some of these vampires were old and wrinkled. She'd had no awareness that there were aged vampires.

Jackie Nixon opened her mouth, but hesitated to speak, her mind racing. Maybe her perception of vampires had been wrong all this time; based on romantic fantasies of beautiful people frozen in time, like in the movies. The reality was, that these vampires were imperfect, after all. *And if they have these obvious physical imperfections, what if they are imperfect or ineffectual in other—*

"Command!" whispered Romeo behind her. "True intent and laser-sharp focus."

She gathered herself and focused her attention, beaming her mind and her gaze across the crowds below, truly believing herself to connect with and affect every one of the stultified minds of those who had been dead or asleep for so long.

Then, she cleared her throat, pulled back her shoulders, took a deep breath and spoke loudly: "Vampire legions!" Her voice projected far across the Darkness. "As your queen, I command you to go forth out of the Darkness, into the earth realm, and defeat the human creatures."

She paused, and the vampires below remained impassive—their bodies immobile and their faces expressionless. *Are they taking any notice?*

She drew in a long breath again and shouted: "Have no mercy! Kill or convert sufficient numbers to convince humanity that there is no escape and no hope in resistance! On my behalf, in my name and in my power, I command you: GO!"

For a long, terrible second, nothing happened, and Jackie felt a wave of panic flood through her, rising from her chest to her throat and flushing her face.

Then the vampires below began to move, and as they shook off the dust and cobwebs of centuries, and then stood erect, their shoulders back, the clouds of gray hanging in the air for a few seconds before they settled on the ground.

As if by magic, the vampires began to glow and shine, their faces becoming imbued with color, their ragged clothing renewed as if new, and sporting the fashion of many centuries ago, as befitted their time of dying or sleeping. Embroidered waistcoats, black velvet frock-coats, silk cravats, satin britches to the knee, fine white linen shirts, polished black leather shoes with silver buckles or soft brown leather boots as befitted their station in their previous life. Women in eighteenth century gowns: high-waisted empire lines, the bodices cut low, the skirts straight and long, their hair curled and piled prettily on top of their heads or covered in beribboned bonnets and velvet hats. And despite the purple light of the castle, Jackie could see their glorious color—some garish yellow stockings under mustard tweed britches, some bright turquoise gowns. Her eyes widened in wonder, and a beaming grin stretched across her face. *This is more like it!*

"Go!" she cried again.

54

And, energized and looking much more human, the vampires moved and animatedly marched in the direction of the opening from the Darkness. They streamed by in their hundreds, moving as fluidly as a rushing body of water.

Jackie turned her shining, manic eyes towards Romeo. "It worked!"

"Yes," Romeo nodded, uneasily.

CHAPTER 12

With their skin still humming with warmth from their night of frenzied lovemaking, William McConnellson III and Natasha Thayer were out in her car, driving to Melas.

"You don't get to run away from me this time." Natasha had smiled wryly, grabbing her sunglasses and pushing them on top of her head before taking his hand and leading him out of the front door, her car keys in her other hand. "I'm coming with you. In fact, we'll take my car and I'll drive you there. Besides, I'm not done with you, yet."

"Oh, but you don't need to..." Will began.

"I know that," she said brightly, clicking the button to release the car door lock. "But if you think I'd allow you to drive all the way back there by yourself, after everything you've just been through…"

"Making love with you was no great hardship, you know," Will smiled, briefly squeezing her hand as it clutched the steering wheel. "It was extremely enjoyable, and—eventually, quite relaxing."

"Huh!" she snorted a laugh. "Still. If you think I'm sending you off alone, after the long drive yesterday and your police ordeal…and all you have ahead of you? You underestimate me."

Will didn't argue. "To be honest, I welcome the company."

"Good."

It was a lonely life for Will—one that he'd had thrust upon him, and he was happy to take any offer of friendship wherever he could. *Even with a vampire— like Victor Rothenstein.* He thought of the inherently evil but currently powerless figure he had left in the Darkness, and about the awkward unnatural alliance there was now, between them both. Neither of them would have chosen to work with the other—an ex-priest and a vampire? Unthinkable! Such diametrically opposite characters should never work together. And yet, what real choice did they have? Jackie Nixon was their mutual enemy, and they had been forced to collaborate, in order to oppose her. They had that in common, at least. Once she and her apocalyptic plan had been stopped and she was out of the picture, well—then, maybe things would be back to 'normal'—and Will could see Victor as his immortal enemy once again.

"I found some notes about this Victor Rothenstein in my uncle's files," Natasha said. "Purchase and sales notes about antiquarian documents. Nothing about him being a vampire!"

"Well, yee-aah…" Will drawled, his lips betraying his amusement.

She playfully slapped his knee.

Will had grown even closer to Natasha during their evening together. And, with a strong feeling that he could trust her, during the journey that morning, he filled her in on the rest of the story—although she already knew part of it.

When he told her about his brief relationship with Kate, and that he might have a baby by this time, she exclaimed, "Will! You're so very young."

He thought he saw Natasha's knuckles whiten a little as she increased her grip on the steering wheel.

"Kate is a vampire now," he said, sensitive to her change in tone. "But even before she got 'turned', I found out that she was working for her mom, Jackie Nixon. She didn't give a shit about me, really. She was just deceiving me all along. She's dead to me."

"Undead," Natasha said grimly.

"Hmmm. Yeah. Last heard, her mother had her in some state of suspended animation or something—like a coma. They were using some kind of spell to grow the baby faster so they could kill it, and use its blood."

"Oh, my...! Holy crap!" She mostly kept her eyes on the road, but took an occasional sideways glance at Will, which she did, then. "This is beyond believable. What are you going to do?"

Will didn't hesitate to tell her the story. After having spent so much time by himself, he felt that he needed to think things out aloud, to help him to formulate a better plan. So, he appreciated having a confidante to talk things over with, on the long drive to Melas. Natasha listened with interest, her eyes fixed on the road, in a sort of driving trance.

***

Detective Gary Bottles passed his partner a steaming mug of coffee.

58

Rich Vincent grinned, accepting the drink gladly as he pushed his notes aside and placed the mug on his desk. "What? No donuts?"

"That's a cliché. I hate to fit the police stereotype."

"You mean you're a miserly mo'fo who just doesn't want to buy them."

"That, too." Bottles hitched up one bony buttock to rest on the edge of Vincent's littered desk. "So, what have we got so far? Anything more illuminating?"

Vincent swallowed the mouthful of coffee he'd taken. "We-ell, I know we keep calling it 'the Bobby Arlen case' but we both know it's bigger than that."

"Although Senator Arlen is big."

"Right. So, we definitely can't fuck this up with him breathing down our necks. But we're now up to..." Vincent picked up a sheet of paper and peered at it. "...a reported forty-five people missing."

"Forty-five?" gasped Bottles. "Shit—that's another eight since last night!"

"Yup. So far. All reported as having been last seen, or gone missing, in Melas. And all over the weekend of Lex Wilde's birthday party."

"And Jackie Nixon claims to know nothing," Bottles growled. "Do we know that they all attended that party?"

"Not at all. Parents are nearly always the ones making the reports, and they know next to nothing about their last-known movements, or whereabouts their kids were actually going." Vincent shrugged his broad shoulders. "Many of the missing are just kids— teenagers, students, people in their early twenties—and

59

you can't ever expect kids to tell their parents where they're going, you know?"

Gary Bottles nodded thoughtfully. He knew only too well. He was thinking about his own fourteen-year-old daughter, Holly, who seemed to have become a pathological liar just recently. He had a flashback to the last weekend, when he'd had a call from another parent—Holly's friend's mom, asking him to come over and pick up his drunken daughter. Holly and her friends had held an impromptu party in a family home absent of parents, but with an unsecured cocktail cabinet—despite Holly having told him that she was going to be studying at the library all evening. She was now grounded for life.

Rich Vincent went on: "Most have no idea. A couple of reports that some were just 'going to a party'—no one knows where. Others were just 'out with friends'—but the friends have gone missing, too…Still others said their kid was going to 'a rock concert'. Some thought their kids were just studying…"

That's it. Holly is grounded for the afterlife, too, Bottles vowed.

"But for the older ones and the college students—most of the people finally reporting them missing just haven't heard from their kids for a few days. Nothing too unusual for independent young people, but as the days have gone by, and their parents have tried to contact them, or they have missed classes, or roommates have become concerned…the number of 'mispers' reported to us has increased."

"But it makes no sense," Bottles said, puzzled. "How can they all go missing without a trace?"

60

Vincent shook his head. "Who knows? Run away and joined a cult?"

"Cult? What—you mean like some Jonestown situation?" Bottles raised a skeptical eyebrow. "No Kool-Aid lying around."

"Nor any corpses, for that matter. Yet nobody saw them leave, either individually or in their bus-loads, and there's still no sign of them."

"But there's still something off, with that birthday party. I don't trust Jackie Nixon as far as I can throw her," Bottles muttered. "Who else can we speak to? What about Lex and the rest of the band—Belladonna Rose?"

"No sign of them, either. No idea where they are." Vincent took another swallow of coffee.

"So, they could be dead or missing, too?"

"Doubtful. Their agent says they called to tell him they're taking some time off. He wasn't too happy, since they are breaking contracts for concerts in the upcoming days. And a couple of them have spoken to family members."

"They must have said where they are?"

"Nope. Just that they're taking time out. Their agent was most pissed. Furious, you might say. Threatening to sue them himself."

Gary Bottles at last took a first sip of his own coffee, grimacing at its coolness. "All too suspicious. We need to track them down."

He walked over to the microwave on the other side of his desk and placed his mug inside, tapping on the control keys. "You think there's a connection with those weird murders?" he asked, raising his voice above the

61

whir of the microwave. "Donovan Smith, and, going back a while, the other property developer guy—his partner? And those construction worker deaths?"

"The so-called 'vampire murders', you mean? At least there were bodies, and MOs to those...blood-letting from the throat, mainly—like some vampire-wannabes had done it."

The microwave pinged, and Bottles opened the door to retrieve his now-boiling coffee. He blew on it—swirls of steam diverted from their upward travel.

Vincent had continued talking: "But that Donovan Smith case—man! Guy ripped to shreds—that was fuckin' inhuman. No idea what happened there. Like he'd gone through a mincing machine, so it isn't even related to those how those other bodies died, with all the neat little holes in the throat. But no—weirdly, to all intents and purposes, these disappearances are nothing like those murders."

"We're like—I don't know—Death Valley or something," said Bottles, taking a tentative sip. "Yow! Too hot!" he winced as the scalding coffee burnt him.

***

"And this vampire, Victor, you say he told you—psychically—that you have to destroy the house?" Natasha asked, when Will had finished explaining the whole situation.

"Yes, although he didn't actually say how." Will watched the landscape whizz past, staring at it without actually seeing anything—all was a blur.

"Hmmm," Natasha considered, her hands still gripping the steering wheel tightly. "It *is* traditional to burn down such places, but given the very particular nature of this house, and the intensity of its pure evil—I think it needs something more than that…"

Will gave her a second look, mildly surprised to hear that she knew about such things. "What do you suggest?"

"Well, given the house's composition—the fact that souls are encased in stones that are built into the very concrete of its foundations," she said, as she drove onwards. "I reckon that destruction by fire wouldn't really touch it."

"Any suggestions, then?"

"Somehow, you need to shatter the entire house into smithereens."

Will's eyes widened. "What—like smash it up? With a hammer?"

Natasha snorted with laughter. "Much as I'd love to see you stripped to the waste, toiling over a sledgehammer for days, there are easier ways to destroy a house in one fell swoop…"

"Bomb it? Or blast it?"

She shrugged. "If that's at all possible. You need a sudden, all-encompassing shock, like a controlled explosion."

"I can see that might be the quickest way to smash the house into pieces," Will admitted, "But how can I be sure that the evil is destroyed? I mean, there must be hundreds of soul-stones in that place. I would have to smash every individual one, wouldn't I? To be sure? I

63

mean, the portal is open there…How do I know it wouldn't just re-open, even if blasted the house?"

Natasha nodded, but she had clearly already considered this possibility, since she explained: "From what I learned from my uncle and read in his books, a portal is effectively an open doorway into other realms—which sounds paranormal and ephemeral—kind of airy-fairy. But it has to have a physical nature—at least on this side of the portal."

"I reckon so," Will said. "I've been through it, into the Darkness."

"That being so, the portal has a physicality in the earth realm, and therefore that portal—by its very nature of being physical—*has* to be bound by the laws of physics," Natasha said, with satisfaction. "So, I think I have an idea of the implications of that, and how we can use its physics to our advantage."

Will raised his eyebrows, impressed. She was proving to be far more than a pleasant traveling companion.

She glanced at him, then did a double-take on seeing his amazement, and laughed. "What? You're thinking I'm not just a pretty face? Or, as I would believe of myself, a not-even-pretty face?"

"Hey!" Will cried, suddenly angered. "Never say that! You're beautiful!"

She chuckled. "Not in the conventional sense."

"To hell with convention! You are beautiful in any sense."

"Pshaw!" she blew air through her lips. "Anyhow. You still seem surprised to find that I'm more than a pretty face."

"Are you calling me sexist? Just because you're beautiful, I never thought you were a bimbo."

"Will!" she chastised him. "The very word 'bimbo' is sexist."

"And that's why…I never said you were…one…" he trailed off, blushing red. "Um…I'm digging myself into a hole here, aren't I?"

"Mm hmmm," Natasha nodded, staring straight ahead, trying to conceal a smile.

"So—you mentioned the physics of the portal…" Will hurriedly tried to change the subject, bringing it back to the important matter at hand. "What were you saying about it?"

"You do know my Uncle Herman was Dean of Occult studies at Cleveland State University?" She continued without taking a breath, not giving Will a chance to answer, as if her question were rhetorical: "While I was clearing the house after his death, remember, I had to catalogue all his books and the antique documents he traded in, on the side. And that stuff was so fascinating, I just became absorbed—and some of what I read is pertinent to your situation."

"Yeah?" Will was impatient for her to get to the point. "Go on."

"Well, from what I understand of the esoteric literature I've read—and from some of Uncle Herman's own academic research—a portal is simply an invisible vortex between the two worlds. Like a whirlpool or a tornado, even—and on the earth side of the vortex, at least, it has to behave like those physical features and obey the laws of physics."

Will had no idea what she was talking about, so simply murmured, "Mm hmm?"

"The vortex core is the part of the flow field where solid body rotational vortex behavior is dominant."

"Whoa! You lost me already," interrupted Will, laughing. "I opted for the seminary over college—and they didn't hold much with science there, since as far as they were concerned, everything was created by God. So, classes in the laws of physics passed me by."

"Okay. Bear with me, and I'll explain in a moment," Natasha said, her voice speeding up as she chattered on, enthusiastically. "But the laws of physics mean that where a vortex line ends—at the surface of its boundary, the pressure lowers. And that effect can also pull in other matter from the surface into its core."

Will frowned. "But what does that mean?"

"If you shatter the balance of pressure—maybe through an explosion in the house, and you blur the boundary line between the vortex itself and normal air— it will set off a chain reaction that results in the portal— with its opening in Jackie Nixon's home—becoming the sort of vortex that sucks the entire mansion down into the Darkness."

"Really?" exclaimed Will, his eyes wide and excited by the possibilities this presented. "Basically—the whole of the Madison House will disappear, lock, stock and barrel, swept up into the vortex and down into the Darkness?"

"Yup."

"Let's do it."

***

66

Detective Rich Vincent tipped back his head and drained the warm coffee from his mug into his mouth. "Yerk!" he spat, picking at his tongue. "You used that real coffee stuff again, didn't you?"

Gary Bottles gazed at him blankly.

"Yeah, I know, I'm a philistine," Vincent muttered. "But when I have a cup of coffee, I like to drink a cup of coffee. Not get a mouthful of rats' droppings and wood shavings and shit at the end."

"Once word gets out nationally, the media will be all over us and the Feds are gonna step in."

"Over a cup of coffee?" Vincent spluttered.

Bottles gave him a hard stare, beneath his blond eyebrows. "Over forty-five missing people, on top of several deaths here, in macabre and mysterious circumstances."

"Don't know…" Vincent's mouth twisted with doubt. "Jackie Nixon is one hell of a powerful woman. She owns most of the businesses round here—including the newspaper."

"But she doesn't own the Senate," warned Bottles. "And, now that we still have no leads or results, Senator Arlen is going to be really breathing fire. He will be on our backs, riding us hard till we come up with answers. Something's got to give."

"Or someone. Jackie Nixon, the Belladonna Rose band-members…"

"Just got to make sure we're not the ones who fold under the heat," said Bottles, cradling his mug of boiling coffee in his hands. He stared down into its murky depths. "This is still hotter than hell."

67

***

As they journeyed onwards, William was increasingly impressed by Natasha, thanking the heavens that he'd had an unaccountable urge to visit her. Maybe this had been a message from God—that he needed to involve Natasha more closely. That she could help. That she was an angel in disguise. Although he had spent many hours in the police cell, trying to come up with plans, it really helped to have someone point out the pitfalls, and find alternative solutions. And Natasha had all kinds of useful knowledge that was way beyond Will's.

We make a great team, he thought.

But then again, he'd thought that about himself and Kate. And see how that had turned out—with deceit and betrayal. *Maybe I just fall too easily in love.*

"So, given that neither of us have a bomb in our luggage…" Natasha began. "How do we blow the house up?"

"Can we Google 'bomb-making'?" Will suggested, only half-joking. He would have resorted to that, if he needed to.

Natasha laughed. "I'm sure we could. Except we don't have time to source the ingredients, or even to make one, I presume. Time is of the essence."

She paused, and Will gazed again out of the passenger window, as the green landscape flashed by.

"We could use some ready-made explosives…" Natasha said, brightly. "Any clue where we might get our hands on something like that?"

Will pondered, racking his memories, but Natasha immediately helped him out by asking, "Is there a mine or anything around there?"

Runners Ridge! Will shuddered, experiencing a flashback of the abandoned mine and the chaos that had surrounded it a few years before. It only took seconds, but he suddenly recalled those days when his aunt and adoptive uncle—the only father figure he'd had—were alive. The only family he'd had. Now dead. Their baby—dead. But those times in Melas, terrifying as they were, made Will feel that he was truly part of a family unit, with brave souls by his side who felt like heroes to him. They had all had to battle with the ghouls rising from the depths of the mine near Melas on Dark Hollow Road. They had won…that time.

"Is there?" repeated Natasha, bringing him out of his trance. "A mine? Anything like that?"

"An old disused mine. Not an active one…" Will murmured. "Not sure if there would be anything left there, now. It's been years…" He fell into deep thought again, only the sound of the car engine breaking the silence.

Natasha shot him a look. "You okay?" She turned her attention back to the road ahead.

Will sighed, "Yeah."

"So…it's doubtful there's any explosives left there in the mine, then. Any other ideas where we might find anything? Dynamite, gelignite, TNT, plutonium 239— I'm not prissy or particular which type…"

Will gave a wry snigger. "Well, one thing in our favor is that the entire goddamned town is a construction site, since it was destroyed by floods." He paused, only

69

for a second. "Thinking about it, I'm sure I recall that part of the construction work involved blasting out lake-bed mud to make bricks or other building materials."

"Sounds promising," smiled Natasha. "If there was any blasting going on locally—either in a quarry for stone, or the lake-bed, as you say—to provide local materials, there's certain to be loads of dynamite or some such, lying about that will do the job."

Will chuckled to himself, amused by the matter of-fact way in which she was talking about stealing explosives, blowing up a mansion and saving the world. He added, "In fact, it was a condition Jackie Nixon made. That's how they got the soul-stones built into her mansion—made from the ashes and bone-dust of people killed in the recent fires and floods...buried in the mud under the lake."

"Very nice," Natasha said, primly. "That Jackie Nixon woman must have a very particular sense of style where building and interior design are concerned. Well, call me an old-fashioned iconoclast, but I'm quite simply going to blast that house to hell."

CHAPTER 13

The vampire army, having progressed from their days as a shambling rag-tag bunch of undead wanderers staggering mindlessly to the castle, now walked proudly upright in apparently full consciousness. Dressed in their ancient finery and their ragged suits and dresses, they continued marching slowly, silently, and purposefully through the pitch black of the Darkness, heading in the direction of the portal to the earth realm.

Jackie Nixon beamed a manic grin, flushed and exhilarated by the sight of the previously zombified vampires now animated at last, moving steadily towards the portal opening, and on, to her darkened destiny. She stood with Romeo Luiz on the balcony of the castle, watching them walk onwards, all with one mind—one intention: to invade the earth and fulfil Jackie Nixon's desire to overcome humankind and leave the world in her thrall.

Once the vampire invasion was complete, she would be ruler of earth and all humanity—not just of the vampires in this black, dead land of tortured souls. And she couldn't wait!

"Ha ha ha ha!" she roared, throwing her head back, laughing like a pantomime villain—a Disney movie's wicked queen. A cartoon caricature.

71

Romeo Luiz edged away from Jackie and her wild, staring eyes that seemed glazed with a lust for power. He shifted uneasily from one foot to another, his own smile frozen on his face.

She is becoming crazier by the minute, he thought to himself.

"And now it begins!" Jackie hissed, rubbing her hands together.

The vampires, in their hundreds, had left the eerie purple shadows of the castle and plunged into the black Darkness. One by one, they filtered into the bank of nothingness, disappearing into the impenetrable shade, until...they didn't.

Romeo was the first to notice. He peered forward, pressing his hips into the crumbling masonry of the parapet and clutching the coping stones with his fingers to ensure he didn't overbalance.

What the...?

He leant over the small wall, straining his eyes to look down and across at something that had caught his attention. It was impossible to see beyond the boundary of the castle's purple illumination, the edge of which marked the full Darkness in which the fortress sat, a glowing oasis in a black desert. Although his sight was limited, he didn't like what he saw.

The vampires had slowed, and those at the boundary of purple light, on the edge of the black and heading into the pitch Darkness, had unaccountably come to a stop. They bumped into one another, as if trying to walk into the backs of a crowd at a stadium, then stood helplessly still.

"What are you doing?" said Jackie, striding towards the edge, staring in the direction of Romeo's terrified glare. "What's happened?"

"I don't know," Romeo gasped. "They seem to have stopped."

"What?" she screamed. "Why? I have not authorized that!"

Romeo licked his lips, sweat have broken out on his upper lip. "It may be nothing. Perhaps we have reached capacity and they are queuing to go through the portal."

"What the hell?" Jackie's voice was deep and threatening—more of a growl than anything human. "What is this? Politely lining up? Is a doorkeeper preventing their passage? Is a customs officer checking their passports?" Jackie waved her arms with a flourish as she shouted, in exasperation. "This is madness! They should be flying out!"

Romeo nodded. It was true. The vampires were not constricted by either human form nor human formalities. They could easily have taken their swifter shape, as bats, and flown through the Darkness, out of the portal, and into the earth realm, as Jackie herself had done many times before.

Romeo quickly assured her: "I will go and find out."

"You better!" Jackie snarled.

Romeo thundered down the stone staircase, taking the worn steps two at a time, and ran as fast as he could through the purple gloom, towards the few vampire figures that remained in sight. By now, the vampires on the edge of the Darkness had stopped moving altogether. Romeo sprinted over the four hundred yards' expanse of ground between the castle walls and the edge of the full

73

black Darkness, his heart beating fast from exertion and his throat growing increasingly raw, through his constant gasping breaths of the fetid air. As soon as he approached the vampires, his anxiety grew. They stood stock-still, definitely—just a handful of them still visible in the purple light. The rest of them, in front of these stragglers, were just vague figures and shadowy statues, crowded into the edge of the black. Beyond that, there were presumably hordes more, but it was impossible to know what was blocking them.

Romeo's chest was tight from running hard, but moreover, he had physical sensations from his rising levels of stress. He had the feeling of adrenalin shooting through his veins, which added to the strain after running, that made his limbs ache.

Panting, Romeo unconsciously wiped the sweat from his brow, dismissive of his own discomfort, because he was far more concerned by what he was seeing. Yes, they had stopped walking, but it was worse than that.

Glancing from one ancient male vampire's face, creased with dust, to that of a young, handsome youth, and then looking over into the gray face of a middle-aged female vampire, Romeo's unease increased. Peering into their expressionless faces, he saw that all the vampires were eerily still and silent. Their blank stares spoke volumes.

"Hey, you!" he tested loudly, waving his hands right in front of their faces. Not a flicker in any of them.

Their unresponsiveness and their dull, unseeing eyes showed Romeo that they had fallen into that previous state of somnolence again.

This is not good. Not good at all, he thought to himself, panic rising and constricting his throat.

***

Imprisoned Vampire Victor Rothenstein had been seething with fury for several weeks, all told, and was losing patience with all of them.

Whatever happened, he vowed that he would never forgive or forget that Jackie Nixon had kept him chained up like a dog in the same castle bed chamber all this time—only taking him out to use him for her evil ends. Having him dance for her, like a performing monkey! She'd had him beaten to unconsciousness by her demon guards, and she had emasculated him with this dog collar around his neck that had stemmed the full flow of his vampirical magic powers. He was kept there by it. He could not transform into his bat-form, and he could not use his superhuman strength. There was no end to his humiliation at her hands, and he was an extremely proud man, so this treatment shook him to his very core.

"You are my bitch," she had sneered, soon after entrapping him and imprisoning him there.

When I get out of here—I will destroy her! he fumed. *She REALLY doesn't know who she's dealing with.*

Victor only had his thoughts left inviolate. His mental abilities were still intact, even if this imprisonment kept his body in check. He could not escape without help, and until then, he was stuck here, a slave to Jackie Nixon. His only hope of escape, and the only vampiric power remaining to him, was that of psychic communication.

75

Through his one practicable vampire spell—related to that power he had left—he had entrusted one human with this ability, too, and given this power to Will, so he could speak with him... *When he lets me through!* he grumbled.

Victor Rothenstein could achieve this telecommunication with both risen or newly-created vampires— but he did not choose to use it in either of those cases. It would be too dangerous. All of them, as far as he could tell, were obedient to the self-proclaimed Vampire Queen, Jackie Nixon. The world had gone mad, and the only one he trusted was himself.

It should be me, ruling over them! Victor growled. *I am the oldest, most active, longest-living vampire. I have earned the right. That woman is a greedy, ambitious ingenue who has only been 'turned' for a matter of weeks. She is practically human! Without my help, she would know nothing!*

Victor could still sense the movement of the vampires, through his consciousness of the vampires' hive mind, which was how he knew to alert Will and get him to take action—or so he hoped.

Where is that William McConnellson kid?

He ran his finger around the hard edge of the studded leather collar once more. It bit into his flesh and had rubbed the skin of his neck raw.

He had already reached out to Will and told him what was necessary. He only had to destroy the Madison House—Jackie Nixon's home.

How hard could that be? Once that human destroys her house, and her powers with it, I will make this bitch truly suffer, he thought to himself

76

Victor had waited long enough. He lifted his impotent fists and shook them, rattling the chain that held him by the collar to the iron ring fixed into the wall.

He had given Will the power of psychic conversation, But Victor was disappointed in Will's use of it.

Disappointed in him? Furious! I have endowed him with an unprecedented power, and this is how he treats me? With scorn and ignorance?

Between Jackie Nixon and Will's treatment of him, Victor Rothenstein felt completely powerless—that everything was out of his control—and he hated that.

This behavior is insufferable! Don't they know who I AM? his mind roared.

And then, in the quiet after he had vented his spleen...gradually, he became aware of a still deadness beyond himself and his own thoughts. First, he was puzzled and curious. He cocked his head to one side, listening and wondering. And then he realized what it was.

There was a vacuum in the minds of the vampires out in the furthermost black depths of the Darkness. A blockage of energy. An impasse. They had stopped; their mind-signals as dead as if someone had flicked a switch.

And as his quick mind appreciated the situation, a further realization dawned on him, and he saw his opportunity.

***

77

"What do you mean?" screeched Jackie Nixon, exasperatedly throwing her hands in the air. Her face was red with anger.

Romeo Luiz almost shrank away from her blazing glare, but as if to overcompensate for the unease her felt, he puffed out his chest, and spoke with confidence: "We have an unforeseen problem. Once the vampires approach the portal opening onto the earth realm—the exit from the Darkness—they become somnolent again."

"Whaaaat?"

Romeo winced, narrowing his eyes against Jackie's shrill voice. "It's as if something is draining away all their energy."

Jackie thrust her head forward, her face an inch from Romeo's. "Find out what!" Her breath was hot on Romeo's cheeks as she blasted out: "And do something about it!"

Romeo swallowed hard, trying to conceal the underlying fear he felt. But Jackie lashed out one arm dismissively and swept around, turning her cold back on him and walking off.

"Of course, Your Highness," Romeo called after her. "I will simply consult the…"

But she had already left the room, the heavy wooden door of the chamber slamming behind her, echoing around the stone walls of the barely furnished room.

Romeo Luiz knew he had to work fast. Jackie Nixon had no patience at the best of times, and at this moment, she was beside herself with fury.

Feeling unsteady on his feet, Romeo leant back on the cold wall, needing its support. The warlock quietened his mind, placed his hand on his fluttering heart and recalled a spell he had rarely used before, but one which was bound to help him find out wat the issue was. He knew it wouldn't solve the problem quickly, but it would at least identify the issue and point them in the direction of the solution.

He fumbled in his pocket, and withdrew a small, soft leather pouch which held some basic essential magical ingredients he always carried around with him. In the back pocket of his skinny black jeans, he kept a notebook he called his 'pocket Book of Shadows'. It was nothing at all like the esteemed, ancient and powerful Grimoire Tepeş that Jackie Nixon now had in her possession; but every witch and warlock kept their own spell-book, or grimoire—otherwise known as a book of shadows—in which they wrote notes, listing magical spells and recipes for potions.

His own extensive leather-bound version was back in his own house in the earth realm, locked in a trunk under the bed, amongst his private treasures. He didn't feel that he needed to bring it with him—given that the Grimoire Tepeş was here in the castle. But he always had his own pocket grimoire about his person—which was lucky for him, given Jackie Nixon's mood today. He withdrew the book, and flicked through its well-used pages.

With trembling fingers, he came to the appropriate page, and re-read the instructions, familiarizing himself with what was involved. Fortunately, he had a length of thread, some salt in a twist of saran-wrap and a sprig of rosemary in his pouch. He took them out and walked over to one of the iron candle sconces on the wall, standing beneath it. He twisted the lit candle out of its holder, cursing when a splash of hot wax spilt on his wrist. Crouching down, he tipped the flaming candle sideways and allowed the wax to drip on the floor, to form a soft base so he could stand the candle upright.

He knelt down and placed the required items down in front of the candle. Murmuring an incantation in ancient Aramaic, he knotted the thread in several places, and twisted it between his fingers to symbolically represent the problem that entangled them. Then he tossed a pinch of salt into the candle flame, listening to the satisfying hiss, and then held one end of the thread into the flame. It sizzled and caught fire fast. He dropped it from his fingers for fear of burning them. He continued to mutter the same arcane words, then burnt the tiny sprig of rosemary. *For remembrance.* Its pungent, savory aroma hit his nostrils.

He meditated, breathing in the strong scent, awaiting whatever would unfold.

He had a clear vision, which was more of a 'knowing'—and with complete clarity, he saw that it was the Madison House, still hungry for soul energy, that was draining the vampires of their strength. All the way back to the edge of the black Darkness, from the purple glow of the castle to the innermost edge of the portal, the house was sucking all life from the assembly of vampires, in its greed for souls. It didn't matter that these vampires were effectively soulless—the energy from their movement, and their communal thought process, whilst in their animation, was enough. It was as if a thousand batteries were being drained of all power, yet the thing they operated—the house—had a life of its own, and grew in strength.

What is necessary to resolve this? Romeo asked, through his meditation, trusting implicitly in the wisdom he received. *Give me the solution.*

The answer was clear: "A sacrifice is needed."

CHAPTER 14

"Hello!" Victor called out for the fourth time, his voice straining. "Hey! I want to talk!"

He had yanked the chain attached to his collar as far as he could, stepping towards the heavy door of the chamber; but he was still only a few feet away from the rusting iron ring that fastened him the wall. And at least a dozen feet from the locked door and the corridor outside.

"Hey!" he yelled louder, aware that the thickness of the oak door meant that his voice would hardly penetrate beyond it. "Hey! I want to talk to Jackie!"

He swallowed hard, suddenly stabbed by a spike of guilt and fear, appreciating that Jackie Nixon herself would take this use of her name as a sign of disrespect, these days. He hoped she hadn't heard. But it was far quicker and easier than shouting 'Her Highness, Queen of the Darkness.' Besides, Victor felt that he might choke on those words.

He took a step back, loosening the pressure of the collar, which had been held taut against his throat, as he had strained forward. He took another deep intake of breath and roared at the top of his lungs: "Hey! Come here!"

The dark door swung open, the sudden brightness making Victor wince, and a pale demon guard, eight feet tall, ducked his head beneath the door frame and stepped aggressively into the room, his bulk filling the doorway and shutting out the light. Gleaming red eyes blazed fierily from his gray scaly face as he glared at Victor.

"Thank you," Victor said, hurriedly. "I need to speak to your mistress, the Queen, as a matter of great urgency…"

The creature growled, and took a step forward towards Victor, his muscular scaly arms braced for action, as if ready to tear Victor apart, limb from limb.

"Please listen to me," Victor stated, summoning all his former authority into his voice. "The Queen is in grave danger. If you do not let me speak to her—you are endangering her life. You will be severely punished when she finds out I could have helped—if only you had complied."

The demon guard snorted, staring. Victor stared back unwaveringly, and spoke again: "Simply ask her to come here, and I will make everything better for her in her time of need. Only you stand in her way. Fetch her. If you know what is good for you."

Still, the creature glared angrily at Victor, steamy breath emanating from his horny nostrils and mouth as he snorted it out into the cold air of the chamber. Victor kept up a steady gaze, willing the guard to do his bidding. He imagined the creature's mental cogs whirring slowly, like an old rusted machine, trying to weigh up what he should do.

"The Queen would desire it," Victor affirmed.

83

With a final combative stare, and a guttural "Gaaaaahhhh!" the guard roared and stomped off, leaving the door wide open behind him.

Victor stood waiting, hopeful. *Is he going for her?* he wondered. *Did it work? Surely, he would have shut the door behind him if he hadn't intended on bringing Jackie Nixon to me?*

Victor stepped backwards towards the wall that held the iron ring, his chain rattling dully against the floor. He leant back against the cool stone, composing himself. He tried to concentrate on pooling saliva in his mouth to swallow and soothe his throat, which was raw with shouting.

He took in a long intake of breath, steadying his rapidly beating heart, preparing the speech he had rehearsed in his head. He had to wipe away a smirk of excitement and expectation. Within a very short time, he hoped to be free. And after that—Jackie Nixon's days were numbered! He was so confident, he briefly reached out to Will in his mind to scoff that he had Jackie where he wanted her—even without Will's help. But no—Will was blocking him, or otherwise, for whatever reason, he couldn't get through. *No matter. I don't even need him, now.*

After only a few minutes, Jackie Nixon swished her long skirts into the room. This time, she was wearing a heavy purple gown, cinched at the waist and full in the skirt, but with 'leg of mutton' sleeves that ballooned voluminously around the upper arms and tightened along the length of the forearms, fastening at the wrist with a line of velvet-colored buttons.

Has she changed her dress since I saw her last? Victor thought, mildly amused. *Is that her priority? Does it make her feel better, power-dressing? Does she imagine that I believe those wide sleeves conceal massive biceps?*

He suddenly found her ridiculous—especially now that she was almost powerless. Victor almost laughed out loud. He had seen her dressed this way before, but only now, in his position of greater strength, did he dare to find Jackie Nixon unthreatening, and even vaguely comical. *What's with the Victorian garb? The velvet gowns? And that face!* She was heavily made up with dusky dark eye shadow and emphatic purple lipstick, but she bore a displeased scowl almost constantly. She really had become a caricature of herself. She stood with her hands on her hips, scowling at him.

"What the hell do you want?" she spat.

"I want to help you," Victor said, with self-assurance.

Jackie Nixon gave an explosive laugh of derision. "Who says I need that?"

Victor tried to conceal a smile. "I know that the vampires have fallen into somnolence again…" Jackie's face dropped, and Victor went on: "But I am able to help."

"And how do you think you can do that?" she sneered. But Victor perceived an underlying whiff of curiosity—desperation, even—beneath the façade of scorn and nonchalance.

"I don't *think* I can help," Victor said, easily. "I *know* I can."

85

Jackie narrowed her eyes and met his gaze, searching for signs of doubt or lies. He remained firm and confident, standing up erectly with his shoulders back proudly, in spite of the humiliating dog collar and chain.

"Look," he shrugged. His chains rattled. "We both know that the vampires—your undead army—are stuck, unable to leave the Darkness. Unable to pass through the portal. Unable to enter the earth realm and effect their presence on the human world. Unable to do your bidding. And, by virtue of these facts, you, too, are stuck."

Jackie's tight lips tremored slightly, and Victor knew he had her where he wanted her. *And now, for the death blow.*

But, in a flurry of footsteps, Romeo Luiz burst through the open door, panting audibly, and the spell was broken. "We need…a sacrifice!" he cried.

Jackie spun round. "What?"

Victor simply stood open-mouthed in shock, anger starting to rise within him.

"I have consulted," Romeo explained, still out of breath, "and discovered a way…to re-animate the vampire army…by feeding the mansion's hunger for soul power." He swallowed, the palm of his hand against his chest, trying to catch his breath. "We need…to make a sacrifice, a shedding of…the blood of an innocent. We need to offer up the baby."

Victor thought fast. *This can't be! This isn't how it should go!*

Jackie's daughter was still under a deep sleeping spell, and through another magical spell-casting, the

86

pregnancy had been speeded up to six times the usual progress. Although it hadn't seemed so urgent since Jackie had got her way without resorting to killing the infant—so far. But if that was what it took to get the vampires on their way again...Her eyes widened with realization, and she exclaimed: "Kate's unborn child. Yes!"

"NO!" Victor roared.

The two others stared at him in surprise.

Conscious of his obvious desperation, Victor quickly recovered himself. "Don't you see? If you sacrifice your daughter's baby now, in order to open the portal, you won't have the innocent life you need to sacrifice later for the ultimate power ritual—the one that enables you to rule over the human world!" He added quickly: "I know a better way!"

Jackie and Romeo shot one another meaningful looks. Was Victor Rothenstein to be trusted?

"And what 'way' might that be?" Jackie asked, doubtfully.

Victor's spirits rose, sensing that he was now in a position of strength to negotiate. "Let me free of this collar, and I can show you."

Jackie laughed. "You are, of course, joking, Rothenstein."

Romeo stood by, grim-faced, ready to use magic if the need arose. Neither of them trusted Victor, now. Not since he had been imprisoned and abused for so long. He had nothing to gain from offering this 'help'—apart from his freedom—and revenge.

"Tell us, instead of showing us," Romeo stated simply.

Victor's jaw clenched in anger. "I'm afraid that won't be possible. I have to leave this room and show you the way."

Jackie frowned, staring questioningly at Romeo.

"Impossible," the warlock declared.

Victor Rothenstein gave a sigh and leant back against the wall again, examining his fingernails with an air of haughty nonchalance. "Then do as you will," he said. "Waste the infant's blood on this simple task—but you must realize that you will then have no powerful means to establish your rule over the two realms—the Darkness and the Earth, without the ultimate sacrifice..."

Jackie Nixon seethed. "Tell us the way."

Victor smiled enigmatically, breathing hot air on his fingernails then idly polishing them on his coat.

Furious, Jackie screeched, and Romeo responded to her anger by blasting the chain and metal studded collar around Victor's neck with a lightning bolt of electricity.

"Tell!" Romeo snarled.

Victor's teeth rattled in his head and his eyes bulged, as his body jerked in shock. He fell to the floor in a heap, like a puppet with its strings cut.

"Tell, if you know what's good for you!"

Victor heaved himself up, back onto his feet, and stood trembling with the after-shock. He was not feeling so confident now, and his head was so befuddled after the zap of electricity, he could barely think. His vision was completely blurred, and all he saw were hazy shadows behind jags of hallucinatory lightning.

"You want some more?" Romeo cried, drawing his arm back in the air in readiness to shoot another blast of electric shock treatment.

"NO!" Victor gasped, weakly raising his hands in surrender. With a tremulous voice, he stuttered, "I…I n-need to…g…get the Gr…Grimoire Tepeş…"

Romeo smirked. "Well, I don't think you do, do you?"

"I…I know there are…" Victor panted, "…two other…spells in the Grimoire Tepeş…to open another route to the earth that…doesn't depend on the portal."

Jackie and Romeo Luiz looked at one another, hope rising.

"Then let's get it," Jackie said, and clicking her fingers, she summoned one of the demon guards to bring her the book.

Defeated, Victor leant back again, supported by the cold wall, and caught his breath. *When my mind starts working again—all will be well,* he thought to himself. He just didn't know how. He clawed his fingers beneath the collar, trying to alleviate the increasingly choked feeling. His neck had swollen with the pain of the electric shock, and he felt strangled. His head was aching, and his vision was still blurred by jagged zags of bright light, like looking through the kaleidoscope of a migraine.

The demon guard entered the room, holding the Grimoire Tepeş out in front of him with both hands. While he stood still, supporting the book like a lectern, Jackie immediately opened the worn leather-bound volume at the first creamy, brown-tinged page.

"Where?" she cried. "Which spell?"

Victor attempted to communicate once again. At that present time, his eyes would be unable to make out the symbols, he knew, let alone decipher them, but he was willing to try anything to gain time and some power over Jackie and this warlock. "Let me…show you…"

"Ha ha ha ha!" Jackie shook her head, sarcastically laughing in disbelief. "You really think I would let you get your hands on this precious book? Fool!"

"Let me," Victor said weakly. "Allow me to serve you."

Jackie ignored him, turning over a page of the Grimoire, scanning it unseeingly. Romeo stepped forward, very close to Jackie. She felt his hot breath on her face.

"Do you need my help?" he murmured into Jackie's ear, beyond Victor's hearing.

"No!" she snapped, and spoke the next words aloud, dripping with acid. "Because of course, I can read Latin and Greek and Aramaic and whatever the hell medieval Transylvanian language all these damn spells are written in! Idiot!" she snarled. "If you're no help to me, I'll need that other ancient lightning-blasted idiot, there! The choice is yours. Which of you is dispensable?"

"He is," muttered Romeo, through gritted teeth.

"Then PROVE IT!" Jackie cried, flicking through the thick vellum pages helplessly, in frustration. The incomprehensible scrawl of long-dead hands writing in ancient languages, and the symbols and diagrams on the pages signified nothing to her. They were as meaningful to her as advanced mathematics would be to a toddler, and she seethed with impotent rage. She hated feeling dependent on anyone else, but by her own admission, she was helpless, and needed these men. Or, at least, one of them.

But not for long! she vowed. Once she had gained power over the earth, as over the Darkness—everyone she knew was dispensable. Especially anyone with more knowledge or magical power than herself.

"Go on, then," she said, stepping back away from the magical book of spells, and allowing Romeo to take her place, his greedy hands on the book. "Do something!"

"I'll take you straight to it!" Victor called out across the room, trying to hide the desperation in his voice. His plan hadn't worked at all, and he felt his hopes draining away.

Wide-eyed and keen to please, Romeo flicked through the pages of the book, while Jackie stood peering over his shoulder, impatiently wringing her hands. It was all she could do not to cry, 'Come on! Come on!' to whip him into a quick resolution of the problem.

Speed-reading the spells on each page, Romeo broke out into a sweat, fearful that he wouldn't find what he was looking for. His magical powers had grown since he had first laid sight on the Grimoire Tepeş—he could feel them, but he wasn't nearly powerful enough for a task like this—not without the aid of an inordinately strong spell. He wondered—if there was nothing precisely suitable for 'opening a new portal' or 'going forth into the earth realm from Darkness'—perhaps there was something that would 'just do' sufficiently to buy him time. All he had to do was impress Jackie

Nixon, and offer her some sign that he knew what he was doing. That he was better than Victor Rothenstein.

"He's wasting your time, Highness," Victor wheedled, regaining hope as he saw Romeo struggling to comply with Jackie's wishes fast enough. "Allow me, and you will have access to the earth realm for all your vampire army, in no time at all."

Romeo scowled at Victor, continuing his search.

"What's the delay?" Jackie muttered. "Do I have to release Rothenstein, after all?"

Victor's hopes leapt again. "Yes, Highness. I will take you straight to it!"

Romeo stopped, staring at the page he'd come to, his breath caught in his throat. His mouth was dry, and his eyes bulged with concentration, as he ran his fingers down the inscrutable words.

"What?" Jackie asked, witnessing his reaction. "What is it?"

Romeo gasped. "Yes..." he murmured, his eyes scanning back up the page again, re-reading to double-check. "YES!"

"What does it say?" Jackie asked eagerly, grasping Romeo's shirt, and tugging on it insistently.

Romeo turned to her, his face beaming. He laughed aloud in her face. "Yes! There is another way to satisfy your house's hunger for souls and re-animate the vampire army!"

Victor stood rigid with shock, and silent.

"Go on! What is it?" Jackie grinned, her eyes gleaming.

"Blood sacrifice..."

"We know that!" Jackie said, exasperated. "We have to kill the baby!"

"We don't have to use an infant's blood!" Romeo exclaimed, his eyes wild with delight. "A master vampire's blood will suffice—just as well as an infant's!"

Victor gasped aloud, but Jackie ignored him, asking quickly for clarification. "For the sacrifice?"

"Yes! Instead of sacrificing Kate's baby…"

Jackie laughed. "We can sacrifice Victor, instead!"

"No. No…No…NO!" cried Victor, tugging viciously at his collar, the length of chain clanking as he struggled.

"Guards!" shouted Jackie. "Take him!"

Two demon guards grasped Victor by the shoulders, which initiated a loud screaming and shouting from Victor. "No! Wait! There's another way! Don't believe him!"

One guard wrenched the chain from the wall, and they dragged Victor off, while he protested at the top of his voice, begging for his life. "Save me! I'm your only hope!"

He wrestled to try to escape their clutches, but with the collar still around his neck, limiting his powers, and the strength of demon guards, he was as helpless as a kitten in the company of wild dogs.

"To my house!" instructed Jackie, raising her arms and preparing to take her vampire bat form to fly through the Darkness.

But Romeo cried, "Allow me!" and, by powerful magic, whisked them all instantaneously through the Darkness. Before she knew where she was, within the

93

space of a split-second, they had all imperceptibly traveled through the portal to earth, and into the cellar of Jackie's new home—the Madison House.

"How did you do that?" Jackie asked Romeo, still reeling from the rapid transportation.

The dim underground room flickered with candle-light. Jackie staggered slightly, putting out her hand on the wall to regain her balance. The wall gave slightly, sponge-like, as if made of something malleable. She felt the pulsation of the wall, its heartbeat throbbing like a living creature, and sensed the dead souls trapped inside it—still not satiating the house's increasing hunger for blood. She recoiled, her hands jerking up from the wall and gazed in wonder around the cellar, still decked out in the black-clothed altar.

"Wow!" said Bella Howard, lead-singer of the band, Belladonna Rose, stepping out of the dark in the corners of the cellar, in her black Doc Martens boots. She wore her trademark crushed velvet top-hat and pink tutu-skirt, with a floaty, diaphanous black blouse that showed her shocking pink bra through it. "What took you this long?"

The rest of the band members stepped forward from the shadows, laughing and calling greetings: "Hey!" and "Hiya!"

"Never mind!" Jackie snapped. "Guards! Prepare him for the ritual!"

The huge, gray, scaly-skinned demon guards dragged Victor over to the altar. One had his massive hand gripped around Victor's throat, so he could barely give a strangled sigh. The monster threw him back on the altar in the middle of the room, and the black satin of the altar-cloth rippled with the disturbance of air.

Still pinned down by the neck in the guard's iron grip, Victor struggled weakly, only imagining what might happen next. Another demon guard took his wrist and shackled him to a silver-colored ring at one corner of the altar.

"I love a helpless man," laughed Bella, her fangs exposed.

"Vampire," Lex corrected.

"Guy's not even worthy of the name," Bella persisted. "Dude has no powers. As I say, I love a helpless man...on his back...powerless."

Jackie interjected. "You can joke now, but I want your respect during the ritual itself."

Bella swept off her top hat with an elaborate flourish and bowed down low. "Your Highness."

The demon guard had walked around each side of the altar, clicking shackles onto Victor's other wrist, and his ankles, until he was spread-eagled. The other guard still held him down by the throat, so Victor could only make soft gargling noises.

"Things you could do to him, now, Bella," sneered Lex.

"Yeah. I could nail him, for sure. Long time since I had steak. Or should I say, 'stake'?"

Victor's eyes bulged wide with fear.

Bella turned her eyes onto Romeo. "But I think I will leave that to Romeo. Romeo, wherefore art thou, Romeo?"

Romeo stepped forward, flicking his head back to sweep his long black hair out of his eyes.

95

"SILENCE!" yelled Jackie, tiring of the joviality which she saw as disrespect of her authority. "This is MY TIME!"

The others shut their mouths, and stood by uneasily, cowed by her anger.

"Romeo," she commanded. "Begin the ritual. The rest of you—have some respect, or you will FEEL MY WRATH!"

The band members shrank into the shadows and stood by in silence, watching while the demon guard continued to restrain Victor by the neck. His arms and legs jerked slightly, but, with his extremities held down firmly by the shackles, he could not escape, or even thrash much.

"š' wm'bd' byš' wmšdr š!" Romeo said solemnly, in Aramaic.

Victor's limbs began to jerk as far as they were able, as he struggled to get free.

"ûma'bādayyā' biyšayyā' ûmšadēr!" Romeo intoned. He turned around and took a meat cleaver from Jackie Nixon's outstretched hands.

Beneath the demon guard's hand, Victor whimpered.

Romeo raised the cleaver high above his own head, and chanted, "byš' mn byth w'nš' byth!"

The demon guard removed his hand from Victor's throat and replaced it on his forehead, still holding him down. Victor gave a hoarse, bloodcurdling scream.

Romeo slammed the cleaver down on Victor's throat, and the vampire's screaming abruptly stopped. Jets of blood shot through the air as arteries and veins were chopped in half, spraying and pulsing out blood until Romeo's shirt, the cloth and the floor beneath, were drenched. Romeo wiped blood spatter from his sweating cheeks. Knowing that a vampire is not killed unless completely beheaded, and that he needed to sever the spinal cord completely, Romeo lifted the cleaver high again.

"biyšayyāʾ min bêtēh waʾănāšayyāʾ bêtēh!"

The cleaver hacked down through bone and hit the top of the altar with a clunk.

The blood seeped into the floor, and even Jackie sensed the earth and the house drinking it in, with a satisfied sigh. Just for good measure, Romeo started wringing out the edge of the altar cloth, to ensure that every drop possible was drunk by the cellar floor. His hands and face were bright red with blood. The floor, however, drank it in deeply, until none was left apparent.

"The house is pacified," Jackie gasped, in amazement.

The floor, and the walls—the whole house began to pulsate with life, the steady heartbeat growing stronger and stronger, until it was almost deafening. The powerful throb of the house's life-force took over the heartbeat rhythm of all who heard it. So, the band, Romeo, the demon guards, Jackie Nixon—and the house—were all as one. All part of the same steady rhythm of life and death—all attuned to the soul house.

And then, the dark portal opening in the cellar wall became more apparent—and transformed itself, from looking like a two-dimensional painting, to becoming a cave with great, fulsome depth and three-dimensional reality.

And out of the dark depths stumbled the first of the bewildered vampires, blinking into the candle-light, from out of the Darkness.

PART 2

THE BLOODSTAINED INN

CHAPTER 15

In the dim illumination of the dashboard lights, Will was repeatedly pressing the buttons on the car radio, pausing with his head cocked to one side to catch what was being transmitted, then moving on again with his finger-pushing, trying to find a station he wanted to listen to.

Outside, occasional headlights pierced the pitch dark as they drove on the blacktop road, still heading towards Melas. It was hours away yet, and night had fallen hours ago. Natasha yawned savagely, pressing the back of one hand against her open mouth, while the other held the steering wheel steady.

The radio stuttered under Will's command. Two-second long snatches of Country & Western songs were replaced by brief excerpts of talk shows, rapidly followed by a bar or two of rock music, interspersed with a couple of sentences of news reports, then Country & Western music again…and so the process continued, in no particular order, without ceasing. The bursts of loud music, alternating with snatches of sentences assaulted Natasha's rears and grated on her mind, her concentration wavering with irritable exhaustion.

"WILL YOU STOP?" shrieked Natasha, only half-joking. She gripped the wheel with white-knuckled hands, her eyes glued to the road.

"What?" Will said, stopping in fright, his finger still poised.

"You are driving me crazy!"

"And you're...driving me!"

Natasha burst out laughing, unable to be angry with him for long. "What did I let myself in for, here?"

"Vampires...explosions...hell-houses?" Will joined in, chuckling. "Good job we can laugh, huh?"

"Good job I find your boyish charm appealing."

"You're pretty cute, yourself." Will grinned, placing his hand on her thigh and gently squeezing her muscles. "Maybe we can take that appeal, add some sexual chemistry, and find some outlet for it, soon, then?"

Natasha gave an exaggerated sigh and shot him a glance. "Hmmm."

"In all seriousness, we'd better stop soon. You've been driving for hours, and it's pretty late. We could both use a rest."

"A rest?" she said, doubtfully, a smirk playing on her lips. "Will your boyish charm and our sexual chemistry allow us to rest?"

"I take your point," Will said, straight-faced. "No. Well, maybe—eventually. Once we're REALLY tired out."

Natasha blew a noisy exhalation of air between her pouting lips. "I am pretty tired, but shouldn't we press onwards? Goodness knows what's happening in Melas by now. Have you tried Victor Rothenstein recently?"

Will smiled to himself. Asking had he 'tried Victor' made it sound as simple as making a phone call. This psychic vampire communication was not quite as easy as that, but it was easy enough—if you allowed it to be. Which he hadn't, for a long time. His face dropped, guilt flooding his face with a blush.

"No," Will said. "He was trying to get through a few hours back, but I couldn't stand having his evil seeping into my brain, so I blocked him."

"Is that wise?" Natasha shot back, frowning at him before turning back to view the road. "I mean, we need to know what's going on, don't we?"

Will yawned, trying to disguise his discomfort. What she said was true, but he had tried to ignore it. Aware of the taut set of Natasha's jaw, and the fact that he didn't want to displease her, Will explained, "Oh, he started to crow about the vampires having stopped...He said they had lost energy, so I *think* we're okay. For the moment. I hope."

Natasha sat driving, still quiet and thoughtful, so Will continued, in an attempt to fill the accusatory silence. "He was just full of arrogance and ego, and it was so disgusting..." Will shuddered at the recollection of the insidious, all-encompassing sense of foreboding and heart-stopping fear that had enveloped him in all his psychic transactions with that vampire mentality. "It actually hurt my mind and made me feel physically ill and he wasn't saying anything of importance, beyond his own appalling self-importance, so I blocked him before he could say any more."

Natasha remained speechless. Only the hum of the car engine broke the silence, along with the occasional whoosh of traffic driving past, in the opposite direction. Will swallowed hard, his eyes flicking sideways, idly following the distant lights of houses and traffic.

"Maybe you should ask him for an update, though," she said eventually.

"Okay," Will conceded. "If I try, will you stop at the next motel we see?"

Natasha nodded. "Sounds like a plan. I'm pretty damned exhausted, to tell the truth."

"Not surprised. Me, too."

They sat in silence, driving onwards through the night; the bright lights of oncoming cars looming towards them making Natasha's tired eyes water.

"Are you trying?" she asked, after a couple of minutes.

"Trying?"

"I mean, of course, you are trying. I do find you VERY trying at times," Natasha smiled. "But, are you trying to get in touch with Victor the vampire, now?"

"Mmm-hmm…" Will answered vaguely.

Natasha let a couple more minutes go by in silence, before asking, "So? What's he say? Aren't you going to tell me?"

Will pulled a face. "Can't get through. It's weird."

"But that's happened before—right? And you've blocked him in the past, you said—so what's happened? He's blocked you?"

Will swallowed hard. "Um. I don't think so. Usually, there's resistance if that happens. He would have to make an effort, use energy to do it—and I would feel him blocking me, but there's nothing."

"So, what does that mean?"

103

"Or..." Will continued, puzzled. "...if the circumstances don't allow it—say, like when he's unable to communicate with me, because someone's talking to him—or whatever—I still have a sense of him, if I try. Usually. But...nothing."

"So, what?" Natasha persisted. "What does it mean?"

"I don't know..." Will mumbled, wonderingly. "It's like he's not there."

"You mean...dead?" Natasha asked. "But vampires don't die, do they?"

"Not unless..." Will struggled to imagine what might have happened.

"But Jackie Nixon and the others—they're vampires, aren't they?" Natasha asked, rhetorically. "They wouldn't kill their own. Besides, they need him!"

"Mmmm..." Will said, weakly. His mind continued to reach out, like fingers groping blindly for something in the dark, but they found nothing but emptiness.

"Maybe the spell wore off?" Natasha offered. "Try later."

"Yeah..." Will stared out into the darkness, seeing only the reflection of his troubled face in the window glass of the passenger door.

***

In the dark office of the police station, there were only two small pools of light flooding a desk littered with files and notes. Gary Bottles ran his fingers through his short blond hair and gave a long, audible sigh. He and his partner, Rich Vincent had been in their office in the police station since the early hours of that morning, sifting through documents and witness reports, and were none the wiser.

He covered his tired eyes with his fingers and rubbed his hands down his face, yawning. "So, we got…nothing, basically."

"Nope," agreed Rich, standing up stiffly and slowly stretching his arms in the air, his mouth savagely mirroring Gary's yawn. "And after spending twenty hours with me, you ain't even got a marriage now, boy…"

Gary nodded sadly. "And Holly's got no dad. Least, not one she'd recognize."

Rich winced with pain and tipped back his head, and his thick neck gave a loud crack. "Ouch! Holy shit. I'm a car-wreck."

He threw himself back down in his seat with a moan.

"Tell me about it." Gary was aware of the smell of his own sweat, soaked through to the armpits of his smart, gray suit jacket, and the grubbiness of his once-white shirt. He was usually fastidious in his cleanliness and grooming, but this one-horse town had a tiny police station, with no shower.

A few hours earlier, the state police had telephoned the precinct and advised another two people had been reported missing in the neighboring county. The growing pressure of the case was really taxing the detectives.

"Senator Arlen's gonna string us up by the balls if we don't get some kind of breakthrough," groaned Rich, burying his head in his hands. "Forty-*seven* missing people—one of them a Senator's son—and no damn trace of Belladonna Rose, either. Forty…fucking…seven."

"Crazy." Gary shook his head slowly. "I'm resorting to prayer."

"Right. Trust in the good Lord. Because this case needs all the help we can get. Forty-fucking-seven young people go missing, without a trace. It's just not natural—so I guess we need some supernatural intervention."

The two desk lamps on their desks suddenly went out simultaneously, plunging them into pitch blackness.

"Hey!" cried Gary Bottles, in shock.

"Goddamn fuse blown or power cut or somethin'." Rich fumbled around with his hands, trying to reach the edge of the desk to get his bearings, his eyes not yet accustomed to the dark. "You got your flashlight?"

"In the car," admitted Gary, resting uneasily, while allowing his partner to hopefully save the day.

"Great."

Gary heard Rich heaving himself out of the chair. But then, something across the room caught Gary's eye—something light and ethereal, like a wisp of smoke. His eyes strained to see. The initial wisp of smoky gray seemed to be taking shape into a misty column.

"Wait!" Gary whispered, reaching out his hands blindly in his partner's direction. His fingers found only air. "What's that?"

"Huh? What's what?"

His eyes unable to move from the gray shadow which seemed to be taking some kind of solid form across the room, Gary wheeled his office chair towards

106

Rich's desk, and his outstretched hands made contact at last. He patted Rich's waist and grasped his polo-shirt in his clenched fist, pulling himself out of his seat.

"Hey!" Rich said, stepping away from him, but Gary kept ahold, turning Rich towards the gray shadow, which was becoming more human in form, although from its still-willowy, smoky appearance, it wasn't actually human at all.

"What. Is. That?" he repeated, his voice low and urgent.

"Trick of the light?"

"There is no light."

The misty shape, far from being a wisp of smoke now, conjured up the image of a human figure—a person.

"Can you see?"

Rich said nothing at all—just stared, open-mouthed.

Gary Bottles swallowed hard, his eyes bulging, as the ghostly figure—now more of a white in color rather than gray mist—glided soundlessly towards them, solidifying in form with every foot closer it came. He heard Rich's rasping breath, as he stood close, hyperventilating in and out through his mouth, but he still didn't speak. He was aware, too, that Rich had, at some point, grabbed the sleeve of his shirt with both hands, so the two of them clung to one another, holding fistfuls of one another's clothing, frozen in fear.

Gary heard a low whimpering sound, and realized it was coming from his own mouth. He closed his dry lips, but still, the sound came from deep in his throat, like a frightened puppy.

107

The figure approached them, and it was clear to see, now, that it was a young woman, and yet, from the translucence—almost transparency—of the figure, and the luminescent glow emanating from her in the darkness—this couldn't be a young woman at all.

Is that a ghost? Gary questioned himself. *Is this real? Did I fall asleep?* He bit his lip with his chattering teeth, and made himself jump with the sudden pain. *That felt real. Am I really fucking awake? Is that a fucking ghost?*

And yet, she had all the appearance of being a young and beautiful woman. She wasn't even white, now that he saw her, up close. She had short, darkish strawberry blonde curls, and stared at him with cold, blue eyes.

How can I see color in the dark? Gary's logical conscious mind wondered, unaccountably. *How can she be a ghost?*

She was wearing jeans, a T-shirt, and a jacket. *Strangely modern clothing for a ghost*, Gary couldn't help thinking.

"Good evening officers. My name is Lucy Westerna," the ghost said, in a monotone. "And yes, I am afraid I am dead, I must confess."

Gary felt a blast of cold air as she spoke, as if her voice came from a cold grave.

"Do not be afraid," Lucy reassured them. "I'm not going to hurt you. I am here to help."

Rich gave a grunt, as if clearing his throat. He let go of Gary's shirt, and wiped his sweating palms on his own pants.

What? Does he think that's alright then? That's fine? Gary thought.

The ghost of Lucy Westerna continued, her icy breath hitting Gary's flushed cheeks, making them burn like frostbite. "I have information on the forty-seven people you seek."

Rich Vincent coughed briefly, and spoke, his voice cracking as if with lack of use, "What do you know?"

What do you know? Gary's mind screamed. *He's interrogating a ghost?*

"The forty-seven missing people you're looking for—including Senator Arlen's son, Bobby—have all vanished into the Madison House."

"Impossible!" Rich exclaimed. "We went there. There's no way forty-seven people could be concealed there. Alive or dead."

"You are restricted only by your human thinking," Lucy Westerna almost smiled, as if indulging him. "You asked for supernatural help—and here I am!" She lifted her ghostly open arms, palms turned upwards. "You must trust me to offer the supernatural reasons for what you so rightly call a crime that isn't 'natural'."

Gary found his voice at last. "Why must we trust you?"

"Because you have no choice," the ghost answered.

Gary breathed out deeply, but his out-breath was ragged and broken, because he could feel his throat trembling. "Okay," he said softly. "What do you mean, they vanished into the Madison House? Where are they?"

"Still there," Lucy Westerna said simply, her voice suddenly taking a sing-song tone. "Absorbed into the fabric of the house."

109

Gary and Rich shot one another looks. In the eerie glow emanating from Lucy's spirit-form, they could see one another's expressions—both looking askance with doubt or disbelief.

"Absorbed?" Rich frowned. "Can we get them back?"

Lucy Westerna sighed. "Doubtful. But there is one way you can try. However, there are other priorities you might need to deal with, first. Pretty soon, the portal in the Madison House cellar that leads to the Darkness." She paused for emphasis, "That would be the underworld…Hell…will let forth thousands of vampires—"

"Wait. What?" Rich interjected. "Now, hey, come on, here…Vampires?"

Gary broke into his partner's querying: "Rich...Now, you know we have had some evidence of this…the Vampire Killings…"

"So-called!" Rich snapped. "And no—really, we have had NO evidence. Just hearsay and speculation. Vampires don't exist."

"Neither do ghosts," Lucy Westerna said softly. "And yet—here I am." She gave another gesture of open arms, accompanied by an apologetic smile.

Rich and Gary stood uncomfortably by, each of them momentarily inside their own heads, still trying to make out whether or not they were dreaming.

"The way…" Gary said, wonderingly. "…you said there's a way we can try to get back the forty-seven people?"

"Yeah. How do we do that?" Rich was suddenly feeling itchy with frustration and impatience. They

110

needed something to do—something to work on. The thought of having Senator Arlen and the media up in arms—let alone the families of the missing kids—was making Rich jumpy.

"Please. We haven't had a decent lead in days," added Gary. "Tell us what to do."

Lucy Westerna—or what remained of her, simply her ethereal spirit—gazed impassively at Rich with her pale blue eyes, then spoke clearly: "Destroy the Madison House."

With those words, she disappeared, plunging Rich and Gary into darkness—although the after-image of her luminescent shape was imprinted on their retinas for a few seconds.

Immediately after that, the two desk lamps fizzled back into life, their searing brightness making the detectives squint momentarily. Then they both stared, blinkingly, at one another, open-mouthed.

"What the hell just happened?" gasped Rich.

Gary's face was white with shock, the electric light leaching all the remaining color from his pale skin. "I have no idea."

CHAPTER 16

Will and Natasha stepped up the wooden stoop to the front door of the Crossroads Inn.

"Hope this isn't like The Bates Motel," Natasha muttered.

From the roadway, they had spotted the swinging sign in the front that said, 'Rooms Vacant' and gratefully pulled into the driveway outside the inauspicious-looking tavern, where a couple of large trucks and a handful of cars were parked in the dirt bowl that served as a parking lot.

Will pushed the brown, paint-chipped front door, holding it open for Natasha.

"So chivalrous!" she smiled, patting him on the ass as she passed by him.

"So…patronizing!" Will laughed.

The door led straight into the dimly lit main bar area—an open space with a serving counter at the far end. A dozen or so men in plaid shirts or rock band T-shirts, and leather jackets and jeans sat or stood at the bar, laughing and talking.

As soon as the door opened and Natasha and Will stepped onto the scuffed timber interior floor—silence fell and everyone seemed to stop what they were doing, just like in a wild-west movie, as they stared at the

112

strangers in town. One man who had been leaning over the pool table to the right of the bar, his elbow crooked high, poised to make a shot, glanced up at them beneath scowling bushy eyebrows. He straightened up slowly and placed one end of his cue upright on the floor, firmly propped, puffing out his chest.

Will swallowed down his apprehension. He had dealt with far worse than this. He sensed the undercurrent of suspicion and mild hostility in the air, but whether she was aware of it or not, Natasha strode through towards the bar counter, ignoring the males' stares, that scanned lingeringly down and up the length of her body. The only other female in the place was a worn-down looking barmaid in her early forties, whose face actually brightened when she spotted another woman, as if grateful for respite from testosterone.

Will lengthened his stride, stepping next to Natasha, and placed a reassuring hand on her elbow, asking the barmaid, "Do you have a double room available for tonight?"

"Reckon so," the woman grinned, pouring a beer. She turned her frizzy, bleach-blonde head and called back, "Ronnie! We got some house guests!"

An indecipherable grunting and mumbling from a door behind the liquor shelves preceded a tall, broad guy's appearance from beyond it. He had a bushy reddish-brown beard, and a shaved head, but the bulk of his body and slightly stooped shoulders gave him the appearance of a buffalo. He cracked his knuckles and braced his brawny shoulders, as if exerting his power both as bar manager and Alpha Male– especially with a new, younger man on the scene. He fixed Will with a

113

stare, then cast an appraising look at Natasha and nodded, saying gruffly, "Double room, is it?"

"Yeah. Thanks," Will answered.

"Give 'em the honeymoon suite, Ronnie," the barmaid smiled, with a wink at Natasha. "Seeing's how they're such a cute couple."

The man-monster grunted and stepped behind the door again for a second. Natasha raised her eyebrows, but flashed the barmaid a quick smile. She had the sense that eyes were still boring into her, and she turned around, self-consciously. Most of the men had returned to their drinks, muttering in low voices, but a couple were still staring broodingly at the newcomers with suspicion.

Big Ronnie came back, holding out a large key on a key fob the size of a baseball. "Rooms are upstairs. Room 2's yours."

"Thanks," said Will, taking the hefty key fob from Ronnie's ham fist, the tarnished key dangling from its chain, grazing his knuckles.

"That's thirty-five dollars," the guy grunted. Will hesitated in surprise, obviously confused, so the man added, "Payment upfront."

The woman gave an apologetic smile. "Guess you ain't used to this kind of establishment. But we get all kinds of folks come here, liable to rip us off. No offense. It's our policy to take payment soon as you book in. Just a precaution. Y'understand?"

"Oh…yeah. No problem," said Will, taking a few folded bills out of his pants pocket. He counted them out silently onto the bar counter.

"Thanks, honey," the barmaid said, taking his money. "By the way, breakfast is included."

Will's mouth watered immediately, at the thought of food. He glanced questioningly at Natasha, who nodded gratefully. Then, self-consciously, she turned around, puzzled; the fine hairs on the back of her neck standing on end, and her head feeling as hot as if a nearby lamp were shining on it. She scanned the room, and saw one of the moody drinkers sitting alone, still staring at her, unblinking. She felt herself flush red, discomforted.

"Say, hey!" Will called to the barmaid. "Can we get anything to eat, now?"

"Sure, hon. Here's what we got." The barmaid pushed a laminated menu sheet in front of them. "I can recommend the house chili."

"Sounds great," Natasha said, straight away.

Too tired to focus on the shiny sheet of hieroglyphics in front of them, Natasha and Will were both willing to concede to any recommendation. Basically, anything was good—especially if it could be served up straight away. Will added, "Yeah. We'll take one of those each, thanks. And two beers."

"Sure," the woman said, snapping off the lids of two beer bottles with her bottle opener. "Sit down, and I'll bring over the chili bowls in a couple of minutes."

Taking their drinks in their hands, Natasha and Will turned around to find a seat. Will started walking to an empty table, next to the lone guy who was still staring unnervingly at Natasha. She saw that his face was badly scarred—almost wholly disfigured as if he'd been in a terrible accident. One of his eyes was red and raw beneath, as if he had no lower lid. *Maybe that's why it*

115

seems that he's staring? she wondered, but she still didn't like it. He was staring right at her, anyway.

"Wait up!" Natasha said, grabbing Will's arm, and steering him in another direction. "Let's sit in that corner. More privacy."

"Okay…" he said, allowing her to guide him over to a corner bench seat. "Although I thought you'd had enough of having me to yourself, the whole journey."

She sat down, glancing sideways at the strange man who was still glowering in their direction.

"See that guy sitting over to the right, by himself?" she hissed between her half-closed lips, keeping her voice low. Will frowned, turning his head around, and she gripped his forearm, warningly: "Don't make it so obvious!"

Will spotted the guy—still staring hard, his hand wrapped around his beer bottle—although Natasha hadn't seen him raise it to his lips since they arrived. The man wore a dirty leather sleeveless jerkin, and had greasy, long graying hair.

"What about him?" asked Will.

"He keeps staring at us," Natasha said, her eyes glued to him. "Do you know him?"

Will gave another glance, noticing that the man's face was craggy with pock-marks and scars. "Nope."

***

"I will send them out now to feed on humankind," Jackie Nixon muttered, her excitement increasing as the vampires marched through the portal. "And somewhere

116

along the line, all in the fullness of time, I need to get rid of that minor irritation, the ex-priest boy."

Romeo Luiz cleared his throat. "Ahem…Mistress, please do not underestimate William McConnellson."

"Why? Jackie shot him a look. "I am far more powerful than a mere human—even one who used to fling holy water about and mutter prayers to an invisible God. That boy is impotent in the face of my power—he is barely out of childhood, himself! What makes you thi—"

"Jackie…" Romeo said intimately, his breath hot on her ear. He murmured into it, quietly and confidentially, "William is a 'chosen one.' His destiny is to block vampirekind from taking over the earth."

Jackie gave a high-pitched squeal. "Whaaaaat? Why didn't you tell me this before, you fool?"

Romeo shrugged. "What difference does it make?"

He was suddenly propelled sideways by a terrific blow to his head as Jackie slapped him hard across the face. "Insolence!" she cried.

Romeo staggered to regain his balance, holding his jaw, which felt as if it had dislocated. He wrenched it back into place, a jolt of excruciating pain quickly followed by complete relief. He worked his jaw tentatively, feeling the afterburn of sore muscles.

"Forgive me, Mistress," he said at last, meeting her icy glare. "I expressed myself badly. I meant no disrespect. I should have said that you needed the vampires animated first, anyhow, before you dealt with the young priest—that was the priority. Without them, eliminating the priest would be impossible."

"Be careful what you say." Jackie's tone was threatening. "Do not underestimate ME!"

Romeo shut his mouth and averted his gaze, staring at the floor, his head bowed. *Her overweening pride will be her downfall,* he thought, but dared not speak.

Jackie swallowed, and waited in silence for Romeo to consider his misdemeanors and repent. When he glanced up uncertainly, daring a look at her through his lowered lashes, she addressed him sharply, through gritted teeth.

"Tell me what I must do."

***

The barmaid came over with a tray, containing two bowls of chili and rice, topped with swirls of sour cream—and another small bowl. "Nachos and guacamole," she announced, placing it down between them. "Some sides, on the house. Just don't tell Ronnie I'm giving away the profits, huh?" she winked.

Natasha raised a smile, but in looking up into the barmaid's face, she caught the scarred man's eye again. Still staring.

"Don't look, but who is that man with the scarred face?" she asked the barmaid, whose face fell. "He keeps looking over."

"Don't know, honey," she said. "Just some trucker I ain't never seen before—arrived just before you did." And she turned on her heel, taking the tray with her, casting a bitter glance at Scarface.

118

Natasha and Will fell upon the food hungrily, trying to forget the strange man seated across the room, who couldn't seem to keep his eyes off them.

"I'm starving, so my judgement might be shot to hell—but tell me—is this the best chili you've ever tasted?" Will asked, wiping his mouth on the paper napkin.

"Except for mine!" Natasha exclaimed.

"Oh, yes, of course," Will agreed, hurriedly. "Right."

Natasha then stared distractedly over Will's shoulder, and he turned around to see what had attracted her attention. The badly scarred trucker who had been seated across the room had hoisted himself out of his seat, threw a few dollars on the table and walked slowly across the room towards the front door, his eyes averted from them at last.

Natasha breathed out a sigh of relief. "Oh, my goodness. I'm glad he's gone. That was disturbing."

"Maybe he's just a guy with his own issues," Will offered, charitably. "Mental health problem…learning disability…We're all different. It's all on the spectrum of 'normal'."

"Hmmm…" Natasha considered. "Says the man who talks to vampires and serial killers!"

Will chuckled, their spirits raised by the peace that was left in the scarred man's wake. They chattered and ate, and drank, looking only into each other's eyes, smiling lovingly at one another. And this time, Natasha didn't mind being stared at by a man. Not this young man.

When they had finished, and Natasha had refused Will's offer of another beer, Will kissed her hand, which he had been holding for the past few minutes. "So. Are you ready for bed?"

"Am I ever!" Natasha grinned, giving a seductive wink. And she took Will's hand—and the rest of his body—up to their room, to bed.

CHAPTER 17

From the dark portal in the basement of the Madison House, the vampires had kept on coming, their gaunt, haunted faces and spare, dusty figures spilling out through the opening. Male and female, young and old—they had one thing in common: all of them were ravenous. They had crowded out the confines of the underground space and spilled beyond, up the stairs, through into the rest of the house, and out into the backyard, where great numbers of them stood still and silent under the silvery washed-out light of the moon.

Romeo Luiz stood next to Jackie, his eyes wide with excitement and trepidation. Beside him were the members of the band, Belladonna Rose—newer, fresher, far better fed and less starved of blood than these ancient vampires, recently risen from the dead.

Lean and hollow-cheeked after some centuries of sleep without sustenance, they assembled in their serried rows: Jackie Nixon's Army of Darkness. She could feel their hunger, aching and eager in their yearning for blood, but she kept them waiting until most of them had filled the grounds of the house—and until she was ready.

121

Jackie's very being trembled. She was impowered at that very instant as if possessed by the very spirt of Satan himself—and what a rush that was!

"I know that you are all keen to hunt," Jackie said, addressing her vampire horde from the paved area outside her window. "And, so you shall—soon enough."

A muttering and murmuring amongst the vampires commenced as they agreed and commented amongst themselves. Unlike their previous dull mindlessness, the animation and life within their eyes was evident. They were living, thinking beings, and although by vampire law they were collectively bound to do her bidding, Jackie sensed that they were also individual characters capable of their own decision-making and rational thought. And if she were to be victorious, she was not sure she liked that fact.

"All in good time, you shall fly—but not yet," she warned, gazing steadily through the dark night, able only to see the light of their sparkling eyes amongst the otherwise dark shapes of her soldiers of evil.

The murmuring rose again, louder, and some exclamations were distinguishable above the general hubbub of low vampire voices. Shouts of "What?" and "Why not?" were heard. Beneath that, there was a less evident undercurrent of comments that did not quite reach Jackie's ears: "That's not fair!" and "She can't do that to us…Can she?"

Conscious of the dissent, Jackie cried, "As my vassals, you will bow down to ME! Your MISTRESS!" Raising her arms in the air, the voluminous sleeves of her velvet gown billowed with the movement of air.

Immediately, the assembled vampires, as one, bowed their heads in obeisance and as she commanded them, they stood by, in deferential silence.

"Yes, you shall feast—all in good time," Jackie Nixon repeated. "There is a superfluity of human food available in this realm, as you are well-aware, those of you who recall your time here on earth in previous days. But first—I have greater priorities!"

She looked to the sky and closed her eyes. The air around her became electrified. With unnatural clarity, she saw a vision of William McConnellson and a woman at a tavern in western Pennsylvania. The precise location rang in her thoughts as clear as a bell.

Romeo stepped back, his own eyes lowered, feeling that he had said and done enough. In so doing, he gave Jackie's steady gaze free access to the band members of Belladonna Rose, relatively newly-turned into vampires, unlike the other ancient beings, recently back from the dead. These were the only vampires she felt she could trust.

Jackie looked at the chosen death squad and projected the image of Will's current whereabouts from her mind telepathically to theirs, instantly making her desire for his blood theirs.

"Bella Howard," Jackie said, and the lead singer stepped forward with pride, flicking back her long, fluffy hair, a satisfied smile on her face. Jackie went on: "Take the other members of your band, and twenty-five more of the strongest here, and DESTROY THE PRIEST!"

"Yes, Mistress," Bella nodded, turning to the crowd of expectant vampires, and drawing an invisible ring

123

around them in the air with one finger. From the crowds, certain individuals moved in recognition and stepped forward, acknowledging the call to action.

A sudden beating of sixty leathery black wings violently stirred the air and blew Jackie Nixon's dark hair across her eyes, while the moon was obscured by a flurry of thirty gigantic vampire bats, taking off with a loud flapping sound that soon evolved into eerie silence.

Fly! Fly, my pretties! thought Jackie, laughing to herself, watching the black cloud of strong-winged creatures fill the already-dark sky, and disappear in the night, into the distance at unfathomable speed. *That priest-boy won't know what's hit him!*

***

Natasha, now naked, knelt astride Will on the bed, each of her full breasts cupped in one of his warm hands. He was half-propped up by the pile of pillows behind him, while she gripped the headboard and rode him slowly, her hips moving languidly up and down.

"How come...I'm doing...all the work?" she panted. "I'm...exhausted."

Will leant forward and took one of her nipples in his mouth, sucking on it. Natasha gasped, her back arching and her hips thrusting down on him harder and faster. But having driven them in the car for hours all the way to the inn, and with her being almost twice Will's age, Natasha's body was tired, and her pace faltered.

"Wait..." he groaned, lifting her hips gently and twisting himself around, still inside her. Natasha gently fell onto her side, facing him, smiling in surprise, but Will slowly rolled them both over, until he lay on top of

124

Natasha, taking his weight on his arms. He looked down at her, and to him, she had never looked more beautiful.

Natasha lay on her back with her curly hair splayed out on the pillow and looked up at his earnest face. She started grinning mischievously. "Ah, the good old missionary position!"

"Well, I used to be a priest," Will said breathily.

Laughing with delight, she drew her feet around the back of his legs, digging her heels into his buttocks. He felt her open, wider, welcoming him, pulling him in, and he felt that he wanted to climb inside her warm skin, finding comfort there, and refuge from all that assailed them. Then, instinctively, his mind switching off, he thrust in and out of her hot wetness, further and deeper. He felt sweat drip off his nose, splashing down onto Natasha's face below him.

She lay with her eyes closed, enjoying the sensations of his thrusting inside her; her tongue lasciviously licking her lips. Her own face and neck were gleaming with a sheen of sweat from her exertion. Her breath caught in her throat and she made tiny moaning sounds that only turned Will on more, and he responded with increased vigor.

With a low, deep inbreath and a mighty guttural roar, Natasha came, suddenly. Momentarily, Will's instinct was to cover her mouth with his, in a kiss that was half self-conscious and embarrassed, wanting to smother her orgasmic sounds from the hearing of anyone left in the bar below. But then, he was all too taken along by the thrilling sound of her sexual excitement, and before he knew it, he was coming too, shuddering into her, unstoppably, as if this was a great release—the greatest release of their lives.

He held onto her, as if she was slipping down a crevasse, as if their lives depended on it, and his moans and hers were a chorus of calls for help—or their salvation—he didn't know. But there was something spiritual in it, beyond the physical and even the emotional. He felt transported, and saved, somehow.

He gazed wonderingly into her eyes, which sparkled in the moonlight filtering through the open window. Their bodies still slick and seemingly glued together, he tenderly moved a curl of light hair from Natasha's face.

"I love you," he whispered, his voice soft and filled with love.

She stared at him, searching his eyes for signs of deception or self-deception. "You're drunk with lust," she murmured, warily.

"No," Will said. "I'm not. Maybe I was…But…this is why I'm telling you now. I love you, Natasha."

Serious now, Natasha looked him in the eye and said, "Oh, Will. You're so young. There's been so much g—"

"Don't patronize me, Tash." Will interrupted, his tone sterner. "I've lived enough to know my own mind, and my heart."

"Will?" Her eyes were yearning, wanting his words to be true, wanting to believe.

"I do." Will's open handsome face was as honest as she'd ever seen. "I love you, Tash. Truly."

She stared at him blankly. Then, a slow smile crept over her face, until she was beaming. "Do you know? I think I love you, too."

"I'll take that," Will nodded. "If that's all you've got at the moment."

"Okay," she admitted. "You got me. Love you!"

They laughed into one another's faces, delirious and hugging closely in complete joy. Then, they kissed deeply and passionately, but without lust—all of that had been spent. Will pulled back and kissed her again, this time chastely, on the lips. They smiled into one another's eyes, and then Natasha swallowed, licking her dry lips again, distracted.

"If you really loved me, though—you would get me a drink," Natasha laughed.

"Thought you didn't want one?"

"That was before I worked up such a thirst," she smiled.

Will gave a mock groan and asked plaintively. "You mean I have to get myself all dressed and go down to the bar to get you a drink?"

Natasha shrugged. "Unless you go naked."

"Hmm…" Will heaved himself out of bed and reached for the clothing they had tossed on the floor and started getting himself dressed. He pulled his shirt over his head. "The things I do for love."

"I'll be right here waiting for you, baby," Natasha said, lazily patting the bed. "Unless, that is…I've fallen asleep."

"Hmmm…Alright for some folks."

Her eyes were already half-closed, and she stifled a yawn.

He laughed, zipping up his pants while he slipped his feet one by one into the shoes he had taken off without untying them. He struggled, kicking the toes

127

onto the floor in an attempt to squeeze his heels in. He hopped to recover his balance, hooking one finger into the heel of one and pulling it up over his foot.

"You'll break the backs of those shoes," Natasha yawned. "Lazy."

Will laughed. "I'll be right back…if you can wait."

"If I'm asleep when you get back, feed me my beer intravenously."

Will chuckled as he closed the door behind him and ran lightly down the stairs.

The bar was still busy, and Will was gratified to notice that the sound of the jukebox and the chattering of gruff voices and the clink of glasses was sufficient to obscure the sound of their lovemaking upstairs. He blushed at the thought.

The barmaid stood at the other end of the bar pouring a draft beer. As Will leaned against the bar waiting for his turn to be served, his eye was distracted by the sight of the scarred trucker again, standing near the front door, his feet apart, his weight stable and steady, and his hands on his hips.

There was something familiar about his stance. He had a presence, even. Will frowned, squinting to try to focus on his face. But it was his gesture, and the posing of his body as he stood framed by the doorway, that really caught his attention.

The man stood strong and upright, and beckoned him towards him with one hand—clearly and definitely. Urgently, almost. Something about the man's confident and assuring posture made Will walk towards him. As soon as he moved, the man walked hurriedly outside, and Will followed him a few yards across the parking lot towards his truck, curiously compelled.

Outside in the quiet night air, the trucker placed his hand on the truck door and turned to Will, crying out, "Get in my truck, Will, before it's too late!"

"What?" asked Will puzzled. "Nah. No…I don't know who you are, but…"

Suddenly, the sky went black, and the beating of a great many wings sounded through the stillness. Will stood appalled, open-mouthed, staring upwards as a great many bats converged in the sky and dived down upon the Crossroads Inn, flying in through the open upstairs window—which Will realized, with horror, was the window of their bedroom, where Natasha lay waiting for him.

"Natasha!" he cried, and made to run back inside the inn, but the trucker grabbed him by the shoulder and held him back.

"Will! No! We've got to go! It's too late to save her!" he shouted, his grip piercing to Will's bone.

"Get off!" Will shook himself free and ran across the lot, leaping the steps onto the wooden porchway, and bursting through the front door.

What he smelt, heard and saw stopped him dead in his tracks. First, was the unmistakeable, ferric scent of blood which hit him like a wall as soon as he opened the door. He could practically taste it—metallic and cloying. Blood—and much of it, was washed across the floor. Arterial spray spattered the dark timber walls. There was an eerie silence, even though the jukebox was still playing a country ballad, the strains of its sorrowful melody mourning the bodies that lay drenched in their

129

own blood, or mocking the rhythm of the last feeble kicks and twitches of the almost-dead whose throats were being enthusiastically drained by the vampire outriders. A dozen or more vampires were hard at work, sucking on the necks of the freshly killed, scattered around the bar area. One of the Belladonna Rose band members, Lex Wilde, held the barmaid in his arms, like a lover in a swoon, her eyes already glazed in death. He drank deeply from her throat, his head down, absorbed in his task.

William glanced helplessly at the doorway leading upstairs, but he knew it was futile: more vampires poured through—some of them wiping their bloody mouths, and one of them...Will emitted a whimper, which he tried to stifle with the edge of his fist...One of them swung the disembodied head of Natasha by her long hair, blood dripping from the remains of her ragged neck, while another female vampire followed close behind, holding Natasha's bloody heart aloft, as if in triumph. It was Bella Howard, the lead singer, grinning ear to ear—her diaphanous pink net ballet skirt spattered with blood from her ripping out Natasha Thayer's heart with her bare hands.

Will stood momentarily transfixed with horror, then bile rose in his throat and he began to gag, staggering sideways, slightly faint. With the first tears of distress pricking his eyes, and almost blind with panic, Will turned and ran back out of the front door.

His sudden rapid movement attracted the attention of Lex Wilde, who quickly looked up from the barmaid's neck, blood dripping from his open mouth, his sharp canine teeth exposed, stained bright red. His eyes locked on Will's disappearing figure, before the door slammed behind him.

Outside, Will ran for his life, his heart pounding. The trucker had started his engine running and pushed the passenger door wide open, the truck pointing towards the road. It was slowly easing out of the parking area.

"Get in!" the trucker roared, and with the 18 truck wheels spinning, Will heaved himself up into the cab, just before the truck sped off.

CHAPTER 18

"What the...?" Will panted, his heart heavy with fear and distress. "Nat..." His eyes filled with tears, and he squinted, trying to clear his vision. "Natasha...They...killed her...and everyone!"

"I know," said the trucker, grimly staring at the dark road ahead, driving fast, his foot hard on the pedal, to the metal.

"How?" Will frowned. *Who is this guy?* "How did you know?"

A great bang came from outside, juddering the 18-wheeler's cab slightly to one side. The trucker swerved the steering wheel, trying to re-adjust the balance, and straighten the vehicle up on the roadway.

Will started to say: "What the fuck was...?" But it happened again—a massive metallic strike to the side of the cab, followed by the obscuring of view through the windshield, as a huge leathery wing covered it for a second or two.

"Shit!" cried Will, trying to recover his wits. "What do we do?"

Suddenly he saw the wild, white face of another band member—Abs—pressed up against his passenger window. His fangs were bared, and his expression furious and menacing. The door opened slightly, and for one horrible second, Will imagined the creature swinging the door open wholly. Will instinctively grabbed the handle, pulling it back with all his might. The slam met some resistance and there was a soft crunching sound followed rapidly by an ear-piercing screeching sound. Will fumblingly pressed down the lock button and noticed that the ends of three of Abs' fingers were trapped inside, bulbous and purple, the fingertips swelling like small balloons. A screaming from underneath suggested that Abs was being dragged along beneath, his body bouncing on the blacktop.

Another sideswipe swung the truck almost into the other side of the road, and the scarred trucker wrestled the wheel to compensate for it. Outside the cab, the vampire bats attacked, swooping down in their massive night-creature form, then rapidly taking human form so they could grapple with the door handles, or batter against the glass with their fists.

"What do we do-oo-oo?" Will heard himself wail, all the time wondering, *Why am I asking him?*

The windshield cracked, with an insistent vampire fist, a distinct line breaking across Will's line of vision, but the safety glass holding together. For now.

The trucker swerved, this time deliberately, into the overhanging branches of trees by the side of the road. A deep thorn hedge scraped the length of the side of the truck, taking with it half a dozen vampires, their bodies pierced and broken by jagged branches and their skin ripped by twigs and sharp thorns. They bowled over and over in the air, screeching—a couple of them killed: one through a pierced heart as he was impaled on a tree branch; one through decapitation—but most of them

133

were only momentarily dazed and quickly resumed the chase.

William hardly had time to wonder, but he couldn't help noticing that the scarred trucker handling the wheel didn't seem to be at all fazed by the vampire attack. Will shot an anguished look at the guy's mutilated face—the pocked and rippled skin looked half-melted, as if he was a victim of burns. There was something so familiar about him—his manner, if not his face…

"Do I know you from somewhere?" Will asked. "Where have I seen y…?"

Then another severe thud against his window resulted in a spider's web of cracks running in the reinforced glass, rapidly followed by another punch to the window, which stretched the bowing resilience of the window and a shower of tiny square shards of glass showered Will as the window finally gave way.

"Dear God!" Will exclaimed, as a clawing hand extended itself through the hole in the window, reaching blindly inside. It found Will's chest, and gripped a fistful of his shirt.

Right in front of his face, Will saw a crucifix appear. The trucker thrust it towards him, saying urgently: "Take this—in remembrance of me."

Will instinctively grabbed the cross, aiming to ward off the vampires without any further thought, but a sudden realization hit his consciousness.

Jay Cristiano!

Will had a flashback to years before—when the mysterious Jay Cristiano had appeared as their savior in the direst of straits, when the force of evil was once again threatening the earth. Will recalled him driving his

134

white Mustang into the obelisk that powered the portal of the Gateway to Hell, engulfing him in flames. His quick action had sealed off the Gateway portal and effectively saved not only Will and his adoptive Uncle Jonathan, but indeed, the entire world from the forces of evil and from imminent ghoulish invasion. Will hadn't seen Jay Cristiano since that time—and had believed him gone forever—and yet—here he was, still driving, and saving Will again!

The grasping fingers through the window, gripping tightly hold of Will's shirt, was followed soon after by the crazed face of Lex Wilde, as he heaved himself through the broken window, using Will's body for leverage, broken glass glinting in his dark hair. His vicious fangs were open wide as he closed in towards Will's throat, the foul stench of rotting bodies and decayed blood emanating from his cavernous mouth. Without a thought, Will stabbed the long end of the crucifix deep into Lex's left eye, and the creature shrieked a blood-curdling scream, a loud hissing sound and a billow of smoke erupting from the wound. Will wrenched the crucifix free of his blackened eye socket, and stabbed again—this time hitting Lex Wilde's neck, erupting in a volcano of hot fresh blood that sizzled against the burning heat of the cross before shooting out over Will, spattering his face with warm sticky fluid. The small figure of Christ nailed on the cross was buried up to His knees in vampire throat.

"In nomine Patris et Filii et Spiritus Sancti!" Will cried, for good measure, blessing the cross with one hand, while pulling it free of the vampire with the other.

135

Lex Wilde gave a wild-eyed bewildered look, and a voiceless scream, before his complexion turned a mottled gray, then the skin of his face cracked into a thousand shards as surely as the glass of the window had—and first, his head, then his body, exploded into a cloud of ash, all over Will's lap.

Meanwhile, Jay had spotted an old gas station on the road ahead, which he knew to be deserted, and he headed there with grim determination.

With horror and fear, the other vampires witnessed Lex Wilde's dreadful demise. As their leader, Bella Howard could not take such a risk with her other fellow vampires.

"There is a complication!" Bella screeched. "Withdraw! Withdraw!"

And with a great squawking and shrieking, the other vampires wheeled away in the sky overhead to rally and confer over their next plans, given this unexpected occurrence, therefore buying Jay and Will some invaluable time.

Bella Howard and her remaining vampires circled high overhead, recouping and communicating their revised strategy.

"We must work together, with purpose," Bella warned. "All listen to me!"

To see Jay swerve and pull into the gas-station forecourt, clicking a switch as he went, Will squealed, "What are you doing?"

Jay pulled up right next to the desolate gas station building, yelling, "Come on!" He released a lever and immediately leapt out of the cab.

"Kick down the door!" Jay instructed, and Will did as he was told—the rotten timber giving way with one shoulder charge.

Jay Cristiano ran around the back of the truck and wrenched the fuel pipe hose out of its holder, pressing the pump release trigger and spraying the ground with gas as he ran towards the old wooden gas station building. Will looked on, aghast. He hadn't really noticed before, that Jay had been trucking gasoline—a huge tankerload.

Jay sprayed the front of the building with gas and turned the hose on the doorway inside and as far as he could reach, towards the back of the small space, before dropping the snaking pipe with the fuel line open, pumping away, gas gushing forth. Jay pushed Will forward into the gas station, behind the dusty counter, and through a door into the bathroom.

"The window," Jay said. "Get out that way."

Outside, high above the tin roof, the remaining vampire bats shot downwards through the night sky in a V-formation, Bella at the point of the arrow, their wings beating frantically, but their collective shape direct and targeted. Instantly, as soon as they reached the door, they took their human form and crowded inside. They were so intent on finding their prey, they barely noticed the wet floor and the pungent aroma of gasoline.

"McConnellson!" Bella roared, as the dozens of vampires crowded inside, pushing through the entrance. "We have you now!"

Bella and her henchmen pushed through the doorway into the tiny bathroom, where they saw the small window, open.

"Follow—" Bella roared, but then with an incredibly loud 'whoof' sound, a massive explosion rent the air as the gasoline tanker went off like a bomb, and the gas station flew apart in pieces around them before a huge fire, its flames twenty feet high, shot upwards, burning all the vampires alive with screeches of searing pain unheard above the mighty crackling and burning.

CHAPTER 19

The next time Lucy Westerna's ghost appeared to detectives Vincent and Bottles, they were only mildly surprised—in the sense that they didn't expect anyone, even humans, to come into the parochial police station at 4 am in the morning, while it was still dark.

Hunched over his desk facing the door, Gary Bottles rubbed his tired, closed eyelids with his fingertips, then glanced up from his papers and did a double-take, his eyes widening.

Noticing his expression, his partner, Rich Vincent, spun round on his office chair, spotted the apparition gliding towards them and groaned. "Not again!"

"I'm disappointed, officers," Lucy Westerna's ghost said sadly, shaking her head, and making a tut-tutting sound with her tongue.

"Don't be. He greets everybody like that," shrugged Gary.

"I mean, I'm disappointed with your progress. Or...more accurately, the lack of it," the ghost said, coming to a stop before them.

It wasn't just her voice that was icy. Gary shivered from the bank of cold air where she stood beside him. He rubbed the side of his arm vigorously and shunted his own office chair backwards a few feet, sitting back in it, appraising the ghost and waiting for her to elaborate.

"I told you what to do—hours ago—and yet you sit on your hands," Lucy's ghost said, her steady gaze scanning from one to the other of the detectives.

"C'mon…" growled Rich Vincent. "Last thing you said was to destroy the Madison House…"

"Precisely," Lucy said primly.

Rich continued: "…but we can't just go around destroying brand new houses. Especially ones owned by billionaire business owners and property magnates like Jackie Nixon."

"Especially not on the say-so of a ghost," Gary added.

Lucy's dead eyes blazed in anger, and her voice raised in a shriek. "You waste time, and yet the end of the world is nigh!"

Detectives Bottles and Vincent looked blankly at one another, each trying to read the other's inscrutable expression.

"Do you want ANY at all chance of retrieving the souls of the lost?" Lucy persisted.

Gary raised one arched eyebrow, and Rich interpreted: "How can we know we'll achieve this?"

"You won't know—without trying!" Lucy scowled at them. "Do you have any other ideas? Any other leads?"

"Just the band," Rich muttered, aware of their impotence. "Still trying to trace them."

Lucy Westerna's voice hardened into a command. "Then, I repeat. Destroy the house. It is the only human way."

Rich sucked his teeth, frowning. "Damn woman owns the town…"

Lucy took a few steps nearer and leant forward. Gary could feel the icy frigidity of her breath as she hissed: "She has sold her soul already—and if you do not take action, she will own more than the town! She seeks to control the world!"

"Now, that's just crazy," Rich snapped, looking to his partner for confirmation.

But Gary was gazing into the mid-distance, looking thoughtful. "No crazier than the vampire reports we've received…No crazier than us both seeing a ghost who makes the only kind of sense we've encountered, in a case that otherwise makes no sense…"

"But we already discussed this, G." Rich said, incredulously. "You can't be serious."

"I am deadly serious, Rich," Gary said, his Nordic blond cool shaken into action. "Never been deadlier!"

The two detectives stared at one another. Gary Bottles' blue eyes had become a steely-gray in the burgeoning dawn light and his normally pale face was flushed. Rich Vincent had never seen his cool-tempered partner so fired up for something as potentially violent as this. But he trusted this man. Something in the set of Gary's jaw and the decisive gleam in his eyes motivated Rich to take action, too.

"Okay. How do we do it?" Rich asked Lucy.

"Blow the place to pieces," she answered simply.

Rich Vincent gave a roar of nervous laughter. "Do WHAT?"

His partner nodded urgently. "She's right. What have we got to lose? Senator Arlen wants us to stop at nothing to find his son."

"Reckon that includes blowing up a powerful woman's house?"

Gary shrugged his slender shoulders. "We got nothing else."

Rich wiped the sweat that had broken out on his brow. His mind raced with thoughts, ideas, and their implications.

"You were in the Marines, right, Rich?" Gary asked gently.

"Yup." He'd known Gary would bring this up. Then, again—he couldn't blame him. It made perfect sense. "I was trained in Florida at the EOD—the Explosive Ordnance Disposal Training Facility, at Eglin Air Force Base."

"Hey? Air Force? Thought it was the Marines."

"It's the Joint Service EOD training," Rich explained. "All members of the military—whether they're Army, Marines, Air Force, or Navy—go there. Regardless of service, it's where all the explosives experts start their training."

"Wait—but that's perfect!" Gary's eyes shone with excitement. He turned to Lucy's ghost. "How long have we got?"

"Only until tonight," Lucy said gravely. "After that—it's world's end and then—it will be too late."

With that, she vanished before their eyes.

Gary Bottles grabbed his jacket from the back of the chair and started punching his hands through the sleeves. "Okay. So, you know how to make and set explosives—right?"

"Jeez, Bottles," Rich said, pounding after his partner, who had already started for the door. "What the fuck?"

"So, we just need enough to blow the Madison mansion to pieces."

"Right," said Rich Vincent, scouring his memory for all that would be necessary. "Just that."

***

With a final flapping of big leathery wings, the bat sent out into the world shortly before dawn broke landed softly in front of Jackie Nixon and Romeo Luiz in the Darkness, and immediately transformed back into its female vampire form to report the news.

"They are all dead," reported the vampire, panting breathlessly.

"At last! William McConnellson is dead!" Jackie grinned, wild-eyed with glee. She clapped her hands. "And so, it begins!"

"N...no..., Highness!" The female's face was pinched and drawn, her expression almost frozen in distress. "The vampires you sent out are all dead. The human boy escaped."

"WHAT?" roared Jackie.

"How can that be?" cried Romeo, his dark eyes blazing.

"I...I do not know, sir." The vampire messenger seemed close to tears. "It appears there was a great fire,

143

in a building on the roadside—and all our kind perished. Your Highness, the boy somehow defeated them…"

Jackie Nixon let out a great screech: "AAAAARGH!"

Romeo looked panic-stricken. He needed to meditate on this and needed silence and calm, but there was chaos all around him. A swirl of vampires had rushed forward and surrounded Jackie Nixon, who had staggered and almost fallen into a swoon, and the tall, gray demon guards were trying to make a gap in the crowds for their queen to breathe. He had no choice but to make the best of it, now or never. He withdrew his portable grimoire notebook from his jeans pocket and sifted through the well-thumbed pages. He had recently used the spell, and although he had no time for the entire ritual, nor to get the ingredients together for it, he anticipated that the previous connection should be still there, to a degree. Closing his eyes and attuning himself to his previous psychic spell's vibration, he quickly consulted the book and muttered the incantation under his breath.

What he saw in his mind's eye horrified him. "Oh, Jesus!" he cried. *How do I tell her this?*

Now recovered, Jackie was batting off the concerned hands of the vampires who had caught her before she fell in a faint, and turned towards Romeo, scowling.

"What the fuck happened, there?" she snarled.

Swallowing his fear, Romeo got straight to the point. "The boy had help."

"No shit, Sherlock."

144

"From a higher power," Romeo added. "There is a Holy One accompanying William."

Fangs bared, Jackie Nixon hissed as if she had been scalded by holy water. "Who...the...fuck?"

"It's the worst possible scenario..." Romeo added. "I dare not speak his name."

Jackie threw her head back and roared once again—a long, low guttural cry like a trapped animal in pain. Time was short, she knew—and now it was daylight on earth, the possibilities for them to act now were very limited.

Then she turned her desperate face to Romeo.

"We need plans!" she growled. Romeo nodded briskly, and she elaborated. "A plan of offense...and just in case..." She sneered with disgust. "Also, a plan for defense."

CHAPTER 20

Stumbling down the road barely able to see through his grief and shock, Will was filling the gray dawn air with words. Words that he realized were of no consequence any more.

"And…I loved her. I think I really loved her. I mean, I know I'm young—not even twenty yet, but I've been around. I've seen a lot. Been through a lot. Felt—what I thought was love before…" Here, his voice faltered, and he broke into a sob. "But…with Natasha…she was…" He paused, and cried aloud, wiping his nose on his sleeve. "Good. A pure soul. Actually…a good person!"

The trucker—or Jay Cristiano, as Will now knew him to be—walked beside him, largely in silence, occasionally raising his thumb as a solitary vehicle drove by. They had been hitch-hiking for an hour now, and the early morning road was very sparsely used. The one or two cars that did pass by obviously weren't going to stop for what looked like a drunken, blood-stained teenager and a world-worn disfigured guy who looked like he might be handy in a fist-fight.

"I…I remember. It was—oh, dear Lord God, it was only a matter of hours ago…" Will went on, his face screwed up in pain. "The softness of her kisses. The warmth of her body—my skin is still humming with her warmth—that tenderness…Oh!"

He howled, stopping and bending down, crying hard. Jay stopped patiently beside him, waiting.

Tears fell spattering down on the blacktop of the road edge, darkening them. Will's head ached with crying, but he couldn't seem to stop. He felt the light pressure of Jay's hand on his bowed back, placed gently between his shoulder-blades. It felt, to Will, as if his caring touch penetrated through his skin, bones and muscle, reaching his sore heart. The heartache he had been feeling suddenly left him and gradually, his crying subsided. Will raised his head, a drool of saliva and ropes of snot dangling from his face.

Without a word, Jay Cristiano handed Will a large, white cotton handkerchief, which Will took, gratefully, blowing his nose.

"Thanks, man," he gasped. Will's red, raw, tear-filled eyes met Jay's compassion-filled ones.

In that moment, despite the ugly scarring on Jay's face, Will saw such beauty in that face. In fact, he saw beauty even beyond that, as if he could see into Jay's glorious soul. It took his breath away and Will was filled with a great warmth—a kind of love, even—which, on one level, surprised him. Nonetheless, he felt immediately safe and calm. At peace.

"How come?" Will asked him, gazing at Jay in wonder.

"How come what?"

"How come you aren't dead? I thought—the first time I saw you…when you helped us. I thought that was

147

it. The end. You sacrificed yourself. For us. And yet, here you are again. How come?"

Jay chuckled, patting Will on the back, and they walked on.

"Tell you who's dead," Jay said quietly. "Victor Rothenstein is dead."

"What?" Will stopped in his tracks. His eyes flickered from side to side, thinking fast. *I wondered! That explains why I couldn't get through to him!*

"I'm sorry to say…But if he was your friend…condolences," Jay said wryly, with a slight smile on his face.

"Oh!" Will waved his hand dismissively. His voice was soft, with vestiges of pain still in it. "It's…complicated. Yeah, he was my enemy, really…but we kinda…had to…work together. So, not friends, exactly, but…" Will shrugged. "I guess in a way, we were close. Or at least—he got inside my head."

"But not your heart," Jay said, simply.

"Hell, no."

Jay shot him a sideways glance, watching his reaction with interest as he stated, "Better always to choose Heaven over Hell."

"Damn right," said Will.

Jay chuckled, shaking his head.

"Sorry," Will added, bashfully. "Inappropriate. See? That's one reason why I had to leave the priesthood."

"But the priesthood never leaves you…" Jay murmured, again carefully turning his head to subtly scrutinize Will's reaction.

Will's eyebrows raised, and he gave a slight laugh. "Oh, I don't know. Reckon it's left me, alright."

Jay sucked his teeth and they walked on. Will's head was down, watching himself idly kicking stones with the toe of his shoe.

Then, as if stating a matter of fact, Jay announced, "William—you have to become a priest again."

Will shook his head, chuckling in disbelief.

Jay's simply spoken tone was stronger and more authoritarian, but still gentle, as he persisted: "I mean it. It's a lifelong vocation: a divine calling that you can't escape from."

They walked on a few paces in silence, until Will muttered: "I used to think that…but…" His mind was racing.

"Trust me," Jay said softly, his compassionate voice belying his cruelly battle-scarred face. "I know what it is to have this divine calling."

They walked along in contemplative silence. Jay even let a car drive by without attempting to flag it down. This was more important to him, to Will, and to the world, just at that moment.

Will stared ahead of him, his face burning, and his walking pace picked up.

"What is it that you fear?" asked Jay. "Since you have surely faced your greatest fears in this short life of yours. What are you afraid of?"

What sprang into Will's mind was: *I'm not worthy;* but he said nothing.

As if reading his mind, Jay said, "The laborer is worthy of his hire—and all God's creatures are worthy of His love, and of eternal life." Jay paused, and took a breath. "Look at the birds of the air…"

Suddenly, a great flurry of feathers and wings sounded out from the undergrowth beside the road. Will stopped and cringed his shoulders in fear. The last flapping of wings he had heard were those of the huge vampire bats—but it was morning light now, and the flock of birds soared through the blue sky.

Jay continued: "…They don't appear to do anything of use…They don't sow, or reap, or gather into barns—and yet your heavenly Father feeds them. Are you not of more value than they are?"

Will's face burned. He knew these passages that Jay had paraphrased and quoted from the Bible. He had just forgotten.

Lost my faith.

"Your faith is not lost," Jay persisted. "You embody it. You live it. It's just that you have hidden it beneath human feelings. But your feelings are transitory. They aren't the truth. Trust and truth are eternal. Trust is all you have."

The birds wheeled in the bright sun-lit sky, and Will was filled with a sudden profound warmth and lightness. A knowing, deep within him, came to the surface, and it affected him deeply: he had, again, a sense of that divine light within him, that had first driven him to become a priest. Like a loving bolt of lightning, he was suddenly imbued with a reason for living. He knew what he had to do. Nothing else seemed to matter, and with that decision came a deep feeling of peace. Will even allowed himself a smile for the first time in many hours.

"When you are connected to your sense of purpose, all becomes possible," Jay asserted, his clear, intense eyes staring at Will, with satisfaction.

Will felt his shoulders straighten back, and he held his head high, marching onwards towards his destiny.

"Bring it on!" he cried, feeling delirious with renewed energy.

"Good, good. Follow your heart."

"I know you're right," Will said, definitely. "I swear—I will return to the priesthood. And as for the war against Jackie Nixon, and her vampire hordes—just tell me what we have to do."

Jay smiled. "Battle the forces of evil, as usual. If we destroy the Madison House, we can lock the vampires in the Darkness permanently."

"Natasha had some ideas," Will said sadly. "And we were going to blow the place up. Is that the best way?"

"It's the quickest and easiest way," Jay conceded. "Given the strength of the power it has generated from the souls built into it—it needs something radical. Once we destroy the house, the portal will close. That stops them invading the earth plane. But there's an added value—when the vampires are stuck in the Darkness without an exit, they will have no access to feed."

"And if they starve, they'll die?" Will asked, hopefully.

"Sadly, not—but once they're starved of food for a sufficiently long time, it will force them all back to sleep again—for eternity, all being well."

"Good enough," Will nodded, with a determined look in his eye.

151

"But it needs to be done by tonight," Jay explained. "Or else…"

Will set off at a jog, calling over his shoulder, "Then, we have no time to lose!"

He turned around, continuing to walk backwards a few paces, to avoid wasting any time. Over Jay's shoulder, he caught sight of a dusty shape in the far distance on the road behind his companion. He screwed up his eyes and watched the truck take shape as it approached them, still small in the distance, but getting larger as it loomed towards them.

"No time to lose, Jay!" Will said grimly. He stood in the middle of the highway, waving both his arms widely, like windmills.

Jay stepped alongside him, making sure to stay beyond the reach of Will's whirling arms, and stood firm.

The vehicle, as it traveled towards them, gradually slowed to a halt.

"Thanks, man! We really appreciate you stopping, sir," grinned Will, disarming the bewildered truck-driver with his charm. "Going anywhere near Melas?"

"Nope. I take the highway east at the next intersection," the driver said, suspiciously. He glanced down at the brown dried bloodstains on Will's shirt.

"I was jumped and robbed," Will said, with an apologetic shrug.

And that's no lie. I was robbed of Natasha's life. Robbed of a future.

"Should see the other guy, huh?" grunted the driver. "Nope. Nearest I go is the next town—Evans City. Then I head east."

"Can you give us a ride up to that town, at least?"

The guy, who had initially been frowning, looked from Will's pleasant features to Jay's calm expression, and sighed, even chuckling to himself. "Sure. Get in."

***

Twenty miles down the road, after the truck had skirted close to the next town and they'd clambered down from the cab, to part ways from their driver, Jay took Will to a twinkling natural river.

"Shouldn't we head straight to Melas? Maybe find a car rental in this town?" Will asked, distracted by the silvery waters rushing over the pebbles.

The river wasn't even waist-deep—barely more than a stream, and he could see every color and shape of the smooth pebbles below. The water was clear and pure, and looked inviting, especially given the smell of Will's own sweat, and the heat and dust of travel.

"First things first, William McConnellson the Third," Jay said, his voice steady and serious, but a half-smile playing on his lips. "I must ask you to confess your sins, if you are willing—and then they will be washed away, and you will be clean again. Ready for our work."

Will's eyebrows shot up. "What? Here?"

"Where better?" Jay began to wade into the river.

Still bemused, but following his heart, and trusting, as he had been told, Will stepped into the shallows and followed Jay. He sucked in air, as the coldness hit his skin, but soon, wading deeper, he became accustomed to its temperature, even finding it pleasant.

Jay stood waiting, waist-deep in the middle of the river, smiling mildly, until Will joined him and stood before him.

Instinctively, Will made the sign of the cross, murmuring, "In the name of the Father, and of the Son, and of the Holy Spirit. My last confession was seven months ago."

Jay looked kindly down at Will, and nodded encouragingly.

"So many sins…Um…murder—of vampires. Is that a sin? But murder, anyway. Doubting the Lord, and losing my way—my vocation. My faith…almost. Betraying…letting down my friends…my…loved ones. Fornication. Lies. Other sins. Things I can't even remember. I am sorry for these and all the sins of my past life."

Jay's grotesquely scarred face had a beatific expression. "My son, do not grieve, for your sins are as nothing compared with your value in the world."

He stepped forward, the waters rushing past their limbs, yet not strongly enough to sweep them off their feet. Jay took hold of Will's shoulders, and gently pulled him down into the waters.

"I baptize thee, priest of the Lord," Jay said, and dipped Will's shoulders back into the water.

Will leant fully back and felt the waters close over his upturned face momentarily. Then his whole body floated, his eyes open to the blue sky above. He felt supported by Jay, and by the water, his body bobbing in one place, the waters passing by, unaccountably fast, although he remained still.

"You are absolved of all sin, oh, pure and holy priest," Jay announced, and gently lifted Will up by the shoulders until he found his feet again, and stood, spluttering, blowing his nose in his hands and planning the water off his wet shirt.

"My penance?" Will queried.

"You have done penance enough, through your suffering in life," Jay answered, and they waded back to the riverside.

Back on dry land, Will turned his face towards the town, eager to move onward, to achieve their goal.

"And now, we need to get you some dry clothes," Jay said. "More befitting a priest."

"And some wheels..." Will added, "...more befitting a couple of saviors of the universe!"

Laughing sardonically and shaking his head, Jay gently clapped his hand to Will's clammy back, and urged him onward.

PART 3

THE FINAL COUNTDOWN

CHAPTER 21

Bathed in pale moonlight, the Madison House looked fresh, bright and new—which it clearly was, having only recently been rebuilt on the foundations of the old mansion. It was Jackie Nixon's specially commissioned designer home. But what no one else knew was that the original old Madison House had previously been her father's house. As a secretive necromancer and summoner of the dead, Walter Pinkman had lived on this site in a house that had later been destroyed, but its very foundations, and an old marble obelisk in the grounds were imbued with the same spiritual energies that Jackie had put to use in increasing her own powers.

Jackie Nixon had instructed a full modern plan in a contemporary style, with a cursory nod to the original structure from the late 1800s. The bricks shone with a honey-gold warmth and the large, clear picture windows glinted, reflecting the light.

Most of the construction materials used to build the new house had been freshly sourced and manufactured, although Jackie Nixon had specified some intriguing requirements for them. These curious specifications had initially baffled the developers, the brick manufacturers and the builders—although they had put these down to the eccentricities of an extremely powerful, rich woman with unique tastes. She was paying them huge sums, so their attitude was to agree—not to reason why she was making these obscure demands.

Jackie Nixon had approved the architectural design of an ostentatious, contemporary home, but had wanted to retain some original features. This kind of request was not uncommon, as far as normal clients were concerned. Property developers and construction companies were used to incorporating sections of old beams as fireplace mantels or fashioning old flooring timbers as doors. No one would have blinked an eye if Jackie had requested that an original building stone from the Victorian house be used as a porch keystone for the new building, or if she had commissioned the re-purposing of old bricks to build a fireplace. They even accepted her demand that they use some shattered marble pieces from the backyard to boost the foundations and rebuild the walls of the cellar. But what surprised the developers, manufacturers and contractors most were Jackie Nixon's expectations that they should incorporate into the concrete and brick mixture some unique ingredients: sand from the silted up remains of the flooded town of Melas, and odd pebbles from a collection she had made.

Donovan Smith, the now-deceased owner of the construction company, who had been Jackie Nixon's erstwhile lover, had been the only one brave enough to wonder why this was, and to ask Jackie to her face. His motive was simple curiosity, rather than any suspicion of evil-doing. The sand and sediment that Jackie Nixon compelled the construction company to harvest from the bed of Floyd Lake effectively came from the site of a community tragedy. It was both a crime-scene, since the fire of Melas Industrial Home for Troubled Youth, and the setting of a later natural disaster—the flood—both of which had caused many fatalities. It was, effectively, a graveyard. Why would someone seek to collect building sand from such a place? When Don Smith asked her to explain herself, Jackie's answer was simple, and even understandable. Her answer, ostensibly, was that it was a local resource—and she was all for using local materials. Additionally, she claimed that she wanted to honor the dead of Melas. After so many lives had been taken in fires and floods over the past few years, she felt it would be a fitting memorial to lives lost. How respectful, honorable and community-minded of her!

The reality was very different. The sand from the lake bed was of great value to Jackie and her ambitions. It contained the ash and ground bones of hundreds of dead inhabitants of Melas, incorporating elements of the life-force of many humans who had died in the prime of life: the cinders of fire-torched and flood-drowned bodies. This sand now formed the mortar between the bricks, composed the earthen element of the brick mixture itself, and was contained within the concrete that held the structure stable. Every room: every wall, floor and ceiling within the structure contained specks of humanity—parts of the souls of the dead. Most importantly, for Jackie's purposes, and embedded in the cellar walls and floors—there were a great many soul stones.

Right from being a small child, Jackie had watched and helped her father, Walter Pinkman, in his arcane

160

experiments to encapsulate the souls of the dead and keep them forever in solid form.

He had worked tirelessly to create 'soul stones'—or spirit stones—capturing their powerful soul energies. They worked like batteries, holding power and energy, and harnessing it for a time when it might be utilized, particularly with the potential to create great magical force. A force sufficient to open a portal to hell.

In Jackie's absence, as an adult living her life and forging a business career, she and her father had stayed in touch, celebrating Walter's eventual success in achieving his life goal. He had perfected the process of making soul stones at last and shared it with his daughter. Both of them, separated by thousands of miles, began forming and collecting stones—capturing deceased people's souls and energy within them, for future use.

Thanks to this work, Jackie was able to combine Walter Pinkman's and her own collection of soul stones—together containing the trapped souls of over a thousand dead people—which had been incorporated into the fabric of the new house.

The marble pieces and stones from the backyard were a range of shards from an ancient portal to the realms of hell that her father, Walter Pinkman, and his vampire partner in crime, Victor Rothenstein, had created. They were the remnants of a shattered marble monument—an obelisk—that they had placed in the grounds of the house, over the vortex to Hell. They had managed to contain many souls within the large structure, effectively creating a single massive soul stone. For the reconstruction of her house, Jackie had

161

ensured that as many chunks of the shattered obelisk containing human souls were used as could be found. These were concentrated in the basement and foundations, which were a combination of the old house's storage cellar, together with new structures made of soul stones and corpse-sand.

Not only that, but the floors of the house had, since the ill-fated birthday party, drunk in gallons of fresh, young blood from the partygoers and concert audience members who had been slaughtered and drained by Belladonna Rose band members on that fateful night. The thirsty house had drunk in the blood, and, given further life, had begun to breathe in response. The veins of the house now ran with that blood, making the souls captured within its stones almost flesh. The steady pulsation of its walls was almost palpable.

In this way, the Madison House was more alive than many a vampire. It vibrated with energetic potential— like the sizzle of a nine-volt battery when a human tongue tentatively licks its connectors. Anyone sensitive would have felt a jolt—a sudden shock of realization— in recognition of its apparent liveliness. The house throbbed with a life-force beyond itself. It had a distinct low, steady heartbeat, which was apparent to the most sensitive of empaths who might walk nearby yet was imperceptible to the average human ear.

If the Madison House had a heartbeat and a vascular system of sorts, it also had the beginnings of a sinister consciousness, and even a sensibility. The house itself had developed almost primeval emotional responses and primitive thought-processes, which were becoming more intelligent by the day. Its burgeoning potential energy was spilling out into daily life, independent of any person—human or vampire—controlling it and manipulating its power to their own ends. Through the cellar's portal, built into its structure, straddling both earth and Darkness, the house felt a nagging pull—a distinct yearning.

The Madison House sensed a growing new life—a fresh, unborn soul and brand-new, unspoiled blood throbbing through a small, concealed human body. Although was the body human, or *half*-human? There was a surrounding encasement of vampire, and it was difficult to tell the precise nature of this tiny, unformed soul and immature body—particularly for the inexperienced consciousness and low intelligence of the house.

The source of this life felt distant, yet somehow connected to the house's pulsing need—separate, yet all too tantalizingly close. The house rumbled with longing, its very foundations vibrating with desire. Far into the Darkness, it stretched its invisible tentacles, but there, it was still powerless, and the distance too far. Coupled with its sensations of need and desire, the house experienced the new and surprising feelings of frustration, dissatisfaction and powerlessness.

Somewhere too far for the house to reach, the unborn infant it yearned for turned around, in a slow dance, floating in its protective amniotic sac within the unconscious Kate's womb.

And the house felt the unborn child shift its position, and its longing increased. The house innately knew the extreme powers and capabilities it would have at its disposal, if it only possessed that child's pure and

163

untouched blood, and absorbed its soft bones and naked new flesh, and entrapped its innocent soul...but the house could do nothing. Yet.

CHAPTER 22

"I'll help you with the explosives if you tell me what to do," Detective Gary Bottles said, solemnly, leaning against the garage wall, watching his partner, Rich Vincent opening and checking cardboard boxes. "But what I can't condone is…the other thing."

Rich Vincent stood up, and faced Gary, his hands on his hips. His round face was red with exertion and gleamed with sweat. "What?"

Gary observed the dark circular stains of sweat on Rich's polo shirt, almost reaching his belt but having emanated from the underarms.

"What the ghost said."

Gary couldn't even bring himself to repeat it. It had been preying on his mind since Lucy Westerna had mentioned it; but he had wanted to block it all out because it was so unthinkable, so shocking, that he hadn't referred to it before now. Since the ghost had first said the words, Gary had wondered whether or not he should broach the subject at all.

A vein was throbbing in Rich Vincent's muscular neck, and Gary swallowed. He knew that look on his partner's face, too. His 'What the fuck?' look of barely veiled anger, usually unleashed on criminals they had apprehended who were not being co-operative.

165

Especially white-collar criminals—people with degrees who wore suits and dress shirts, just like Gary Bottles.

"Which parts of what the ghost said?" Rich snarled, wiping the sweat off his brow with the back of his hand. "I'm busting my ass here to find stuff we can blow up the house with and you're talking to me in riddles."

Gary Bottle's pale face flushed red and hot. "The stuff she said about...the other thing."

"Fuck's sake!" Rich kicked the nearest box, which rattled heavily. Gary trusted that there was nothing explosive in that particular box, but he had no time to wonder, since Rich himself exploded: "Just tell me!"

"That we need the blood of a newborn baby to thoroughly complete the destruction of the house," Gary reeled off the direction that Lucy Westerna had given them when she had detailed their task.

Rich looked down, suddenly finding the open box fascinating. "We'll face that when we come to it."

"It's...inhumane. Disturbing."

"Yeah. Well. Do we actually need that? If I can get enough explosives to blow the house to smithereens..."

"And yet, the ghost said..." Gary licked his dry lips in a quick, nervous movement. "What was it, again? 'The house's malignance was conceived in blood and must be buried in the same.' Something like that."

Gary knew all too well, that this was exactly what Lucy Westerna's ghost had said. Every word had consistently rolled through his mind in the same sequence, over and over, despite his best attempts to switch it off and forget the statement completely.

"I...I jus...I can't," he stammered. "I just cannot conceive th..."

166

"And she said she would sort that out," Rich said quickly, reaching down and pulling open the flaps of another box, rummaging into it and pulling out a spool of wire. "We just need to worry about the explosives."

Gary was not reassured. His own forehead was clammy with anxiety. "I still don't want anything to do with killing a baby. Not even to get Senator Arlen off our case."

Rich threw the wire into a pile of other parts—cable clips, more wire, an old clock, and other detritus he had accumulated—near his boots.

"And she said she would sort it out, remember?" He gave an exasperated sigh, his frustration clearly evident. "She even reassured us—she said nobody innocent would get hurt!"

"What she said was: 'I know where to get you a nasty kid that no one will ever miss.' But I can't even allow that!" Rich cried, his face stricken, in pain. "A kid is a kid! She said we needed a baby! An innocent baby—and its blood! How can a baby be a nasty kid? There's no such thing!"

Rich wondered at his partner's unaccountable reaction—his over-the-top passion and concern. His eyes were wild, and he even looked a little unhinged. Sure, Gary was a father, but—the guy needed to get a grip.

"This whole fuckin' world is crazy at the minute, G. I need you to not cross over that edge. Don't you go crazy on me, too. Pull yourself to-fuckin'-gether. She probably meant some ghost baby, anyway. Keep your head, man!"

He tipped out one of the cardboard boxes, and its screws, bolts and metal boxes came out in a cascade, crashing loudly onto the concrete floor of the garage. Then, Rich scooped up the small pile of selected items near his feet, into its emptiness.

"If that ghost abducts a real, live child and expects us to be party to its murder…" Gary persisted. "Then, I'm out of here."

Rich picked up the box and fixed his partner with a glare. "We're both out of here. Now."

***

Father William McConnellson III marveled at how comfortable he felt, dressed once again in a priest's cassock and vestments. He hated that they'd had to break into the Evans City Parish Church, St Vincent's, to find supplies of holy water, ointments and these vestments to prepare for the battle ahead, but they could get no answer to their frantic hammering on the door of the church, nor at the priest's house, and time was of the essence.

"Needs must," Jay Cristiano said. "If the priest knew our purpose, he would gladly give these things."

Will was just glad that he had JC himself with him, to offer him absolution for this sin. That, and the eight hundred dollars Jay had left in the offertory to make some amends for their 'borrowing'.

With Jay driving a rental car filled with gas, they set off for Melas. On the way, they stopped at a hardware store and bought a pair of bolt-cutters and a few other things.

CHAPTER 23

A priest doesn't hate, William thought as the car cut through the growing darkness. *A priest is a man of peace. He is a healer, not a killer. A priest's sworn mission is to cure the world of its malaise. But...*

Jay Cristiano had said little since they'd left Evans City, Pennsylvania. He'd left William to his private reflections. He understood that his young companion needed time to come to terms with his current situation. He needed to resolve both his loss and his restoration to grace. And he needed to do so fast.

William had to be 'ready' by the time their car pulled into Melas.

It was a clear night and Jay drove fast.

Yes, a priest's sworn mission is to cure the world, William agreed with himself. But sometimes curing a disease required an excision. *Take a cancer, for instance. You don't give the afflicted person aspirin and send them home. No, you knock 'em out with gas, and then you cut into them. You cut the cancer of them and throw it away into the trash. The cancer doesn't want to leave their body, but you make it. You force the cancer to die.*

Staring through the window at an oncoming van, he grimaced. *Vampirism is a cancer,* he thought. *And once again I'm the doctor about to perform the curative operation.*

There was no doubt whatsoever in William's mind about that. Vampirism was a disease. Vampirism wasn't so much a physical ailment—even though the undead condition was transmitted via blood—as a psychological one. The craving wasn't as much the problem as the mental change that came over those who were 'turned.'

Vampires weren't the cute, sparkly teenagers' modern fiction portrayed them to be. They were evil bastards, rotten to the core; predators who viewed the entirety of the unturned human race as cattle. Also, like ancient aristocrats, bloodsuckers were bloated with pride; they felt they were better than you. Worst of all, they felt they had *a right* to drain you of your life force to sustain themselves.

No, they weren't angsty teenage boys whose primary concern was falling in love with the cute brunette human girl next door.

William smirked. If either Anne Rice or Stephenie Meyer ever met a vampire in person, they'd both instantly reverse their opinions of the ghastly horrors.

Jackie Nixon isn't human anymore; she's an undead plague bent on wiping out the human race.

William accepted that the vampire superiority complex was necessary for bloodsucker survival. But there was another psychological change he'd noticed in the turned, one that became more pronounced the longer the vampire survived. This was a 'hardening' of the emotions; a callousness that gradually deepened just like the latter stages of a terminal infection.

170

Slowly but surely, the undead lost more than just their human life. Their very emotions became corrupted. Their feelings of empathy corroded like metal left in acid, till finally what was left was hollow, an abomination in God's sight only concerned with its own survival. In a way the vampire was both the pinnacle and nadir of human evolution. The creature was stronger and smarter than mortal man or woman, but at the same time it was as bestial as a rat, pondering only its own comfort, driven entirely by selfishness and greed, eternally seeking to fill its own belly with the life of others.

William sighed. Jackie Nixon was merely the female version of the now dead Victor Rothenstein. There was nothing to choose between them. Lose one evil and gain another, equally as bad.

Jay Cristiano looked over at William. "You okay, man?"

"Yeah, just thinking."

Jay left him to his thoughts again. Their rented car rolled relentlessly on, carrying them both forward to their rendezvous with the darkest of destinies.

William's hugest problem now was not hating Jackie Nixon. *A priest forgives*, he told himself over and over. *A priest doesn't hate. A priest forgives. I don't hate Jackie Nixon. Jackie Nixon is a cancer. In addition, she's a carcinogen, out to infect the world with death. The reason I must stop her is because she's a danger to everyone alive, not because she's now taken two women I loved from me.*

He corrected himself. He'd had particularly bad luck with vampires, he thought. Natasha was actually the *third* woman the vampires had taken from him. The first

171

was his youth counselor Lucy Westerna, a sweet lady who helped him during a dark period of his life as a 'guest' at the Melas Industrial Home for Troubled Youth, who now existed as a Yoda-like figure that popped up now and again to deliver dire warnings of the approaching vampire Armageddon to people.

Remembering Lucy's death made William grit his teeth. She had been raped and torn apart before his very eyes by a large demonic bat-like creature, as he watched helplessly as the scene unfolded on a security monitor at the school. He had barricaded himself in this security office as the vampire wreaked havoc on the students and staff in the home's cafeteria.

His gains of forgiveness almost slipped away, but he caught their tattered ends just before they escaped his heart and soothed their angry flutterings with soft fingers of scripture verse about the importance of pardoning the failings of others in divine purpose.

It was hard going, but he forced it through. It was either that or fail before he'd even attempted the given task. *I'm on a mission of mercy, not one of revenge. I must get this straight in my mind. I'm also on a rescue mission, I want to save my unborn child. But, I do not hate Jackie Nixon. I hate the evil that the vampire represents; I don't hate the woman for what she's done to me.*

Finally, just about the time when the outskirt lights of Clarksburg, West Virginia, the town before Melas appeared, William reached his point of peace. With a soft sigh, he relaxed in the car seat. He cleared his mind of evil and filled it with thoughts of the Almighty's goodness and his protection against the monstrous evil ahead. *By myself I can do nothing, but in Him I can do all things.* While meditating, he fingered a rosary. *The Lord said: I am the vine and ye are the branches. As the vine cannot produce fruit apart from the branches, so too ye can produce no fruit except ye abide in me…Abide in me and I in you…*

Melas's darkened buildings appeared before them in clumps. As if in sympathy with the darkness they faced, Jay now turned their car headlights off.

As they drove further into Melas, a cold smile settled over William's lips.

The driver with the scarred face glanced at him. "You're back to normal now, huh?"

The reborn priest nodded back. Then he grinned. "Let's go teach the evil vampire queen a lesson in respecting the human race!"

***

A little later they arrived at the Moran-Smith Construction headquarters. As expected the front gate was shut and padlocked. Also, as expected, there were no guards in sight. With the slew of bloodsucker rumors everywhere, no one was going to sit in the guardhouse waiting to get their throat ripped out.

Jay parked. William got out the pair of bolt cutters they'd bought after renting the car. He walked over and snipped the pair of chains holding the gate together. He slid back the bolts and the two metal halves swung open.

Jay drove through and waited. William shut the gates again, and hung the chains back in place on them, just

173

in case someone drove past. Then he got back into the car.

Jay Cristiano drove the car through the dark compound, around the empty prefabricated offices. Past Donovan's Smith's office with the yellow 'Crime Scene: Do Not Cross' tape all over its front door. Past rows of parked trucks and skid steers.

The camp was completely deserted. Empty of life except for some cats on the prowl. Work on the town had stalled completely since the vampire killings had claimed the lives of both company owners. All the staff had left town to return *only* once the police had caught whoever had splattered Donovan Smith all over his office. If the boss could get killed that easy...

"Remember, Will," Jay said as they headed towards an isolated cabin up by the perimeter fence, "This is a human battle, not a divine one. Men caused this problem, so men must fix it. I'm merely here to assist you."

William nodded.

Jay parked in front of the isolated cabin, beside two white RAM pickup trucks. The prefabricated building bore the warning 'DANGER: EXPLOSIVES!' in bold red letters on a white sign.

"Here we are," Jay said. "Time to load up."

They got down. The explosives cabin had two doors. They forced the left on with a crowbar. Inside, the cabin was full of crates. William imagined the room smelt of death.

"Load up the truck next to our car," Jay instructed.

"The truck keys?"

"They're in the office next door. We'll pick 'em up when we're done."

William stripped off his priestly robe and they got to work.

"Hey, careful moving that," Jay said in mock alarm. "We want to blow the vampires to bits, not ourselves."

William nodded.

They loaded up dynamite, gelignite, blasting caps, detcord, a spool of cable that was with the explosives, a detonator and a timer. They both worked with great care, conscious not to drop anything.

William was particularly cautious. He was the one who climbed into the bed of the pickup truck and stacked and arranged the crates. Priest or not, he wasn't yet ready to be blown to kingdom come.

"Say, Jay," he asked after stacking a crate. "I know all this is great in theory, but do you know how to work explosives? I mean, how do we actually blow the mansion up?"

Jay's horribly scarred face creased up into a grin. "We'll work it out, Will. Just keep on loading."

"Yeah, but how?"

"Don't worry about it, Will. The Lord works in mysterious ways."

William let it go. The amount of care they were taking with the loading spoke of their cargo being especially volatile. With that in mind, he figured it couldn't be that difficult to level a mansion. Even a huge one like the Madison House.

Finally, they were done. While Will pulled his robes back over his sweating body, Jay broke into the cabin office and retrieved the keys for the pickup truck.

175

They left, with Will driving the RAM truck. Jay drove ahead in the rental car. They let themselves out the front gate, with Will arranging the snipped chains to give the impression that they were still whole.

They left as they'd arrived, with both sets of headlights off. True there weren't any cops about to stop them, but the damn bloodsuckers they were hunting might notice them from above, and neither of them wanted another experience like the one they'd recently had in Jay's 18-wheeler.

At the turnoff to the Madison House, Jay parked the rental car. It seemed a bad idea to take the car up to the mansion: shit happened. If the explosion and possible resulting fire got out of control, they just might find themselves making a long, long walk out of town. Not to mention that the car rental folks would be after Will for compensation for their burnt/blown up vehicle.

Jay walked over and got in the RAM. He and William each looked at the other and nodded.

"It's time," Jay said.

Will fingered the cross dangling around his neck, then nodded. "Yes, it is."

He put the truck in motion and they climbed the hill.

CHAPTER 24

It was hard convincing people of natural things they'd not personally witnessed, less talk of the supernatural. It sucked.

These were the thoughts in Lucy Westerna's ghostly mind when she appeared in the vampire realm. She stood on the plain of the dead, staring at the Vampire city, at Vampire Castle with its purple light. The ghastly light had an obscenity to it that offended her.

It was hard convincing people. The ghost was relieved that she'd finally gotten her point across to the two policemen. Cops had a reputation for being hardheaded about such things.

She was glad however that she'd convinced them. Both men were outside the mansion now, setting up the explosive charges which would level the place.

Good riddance to bad rubbish.

The ghostly Lucy Westerna had no problem with disliking vampires. They'd killed her, and she hated them with a passion. She hated them with her entire being. Here she was, trapped between Heaven and Hell and it was all those damn bloodsuckers' fault.

Well, it was time for some payback. Jackie Nixon— the woman's very name filled Lucy with intense rage—

was going down. The vampire queen was about to discover the truth of the adage 'Hell hath no fury.'

But—Lucy's eyes swept the distant vampire ranks. The numbers of the undead seemed endless. She felt worried for a moment. *There are so many of them! If our plan fails, the human race is finished.*

Then a cold smile creased her lips. *Well, I guess then that it's up to me to ensure that it doesn't fail, isn't it?*

After focusing her mind on Vampire Castle and getting her bearings right, Lucy Westerna's ghost vanished.

***

The ghost instantly reappeared, this time in the upper bedroom where Kate Nixon lay unconscious. The room temperature dropped as the swirling mist beside the bed condensed into Lucy.

Lucy stood for a moment watching. She wasn't concerned about being discovered. She thought it possible that Jackie Nixon's demon guard might be able to see her, but there were none of them outside the door. None were needed to protect sleeping beauty.

Nor were there any vampires nearby, all were outside, excited and anticipating the endless feeding spree their queen intended to unleash on the human world come midnight.

For a while the ghost studied Kate Nixon. The pregnant young woman reminded her of what she herself had once been: young and beautiful, and with a bright future ahead. Her bulging belly—Kate was as close to term as it was possible to be—spoke of the

178

advent of new life. But Kate was now corrupted. She was evil. Her trance-state did not exonerate her of complicity in the doom ahead. She was largely responsible for the terror about to be unleashed on mankind.

Her baby was an abomination. Kate wasn't about to birth new life, but new death. Her offspring would be a tool of humanity's damnation.

Lucy decided she'd waited long enough. A grim determination came into her eyes. She climbed up on the bed and lay down on top of Kate Nixon.

Slowly the ghost sank down into the pregnant vampire. Slowly the two of them fused into one person.

Inside the pregnant vampire, Lucy Westerna took her time getting used to the feeling of having a body again. It had been a while! Like one taking the controls of an unfamiliar car, she relaxed and reacquainted herself with what muscles and nerves felt like. Not how they worked—one never understood that—but just the feeling. It felt like she was lying in a luxurious bed again after walking through the hot sun. Such a nice feeling. She could almost go to sleep in here herself.

She caught herself then. What she was feeling was spillover effects of the spell keeping her host unconscious. If she went under too...

The next moment Kate Nixon sat up in bed.

Kate, of course, was still out cold. Lucy was running her. The pregnant girl's eyes were still shut as she got down off her bed. There was no change in her facial expression. If anything, her previously placid face now looked dead.

179

In essence, Kate Nixon was now sleepwalking under Lucy's guidance.

Lucy walked Kate's body to the bedroom door and opened it. She stepped outside. She looked left and right. It didn't matter that Kate's eyes were shut—Lucy could see through her eyelids. The corridor was empty. She took a few moments to get her bearings right. Now, which way was the front entrance? *I was standing over on the cliffside, which was that way, from there, this bedroom was on the right...*

She looked back inside the room to confirm her deductions. That was the thing now: wrapped inside Kate's body like she was, she couldn't just teleport them both to their destination. She had to 'walk' the vampire there. And fast. Through her linkage with Kate's body Lucy could feel the baby move. The little half-vampire boy was kicking her with gusto. The damn thing was knocking at the door, demanding to be born. It might born at any moment now. The thing to watch for was Kate's waters breaking. That hadn't happened yet. But then, Kate was a vampire; what if their waters broke late, or...?

Once certain of the right way to go, Lucy moved Kate's body out of the bedroom and began walking.

She walked Kate fast. Her main concern was avoiding the demon guards. As far as she knew, once she possessed a person/vampire she could make that person invisible too. The demon guards, however, saw differently from humans and undead. She'd be visible to them.

Her luck held. All her way through the castle, down two long corridors and descending the immense stone stairs, she didn't see a single one of the Vampire Queen's scaly eight-foot sentinels. She was relieved.

Finally, she walked Kate's body out through the castle's huge front entrance.

The ethereal Lucy steeled her nerve before stepping over the threshold. Here was the acid test. The vampires shouldn't see Kate now. Most of them at least. That damn warlock Romeo Luiz might be able to though. She hoped he wasn't anywhere nearby.

The vampires thronged the courtyard and beyond that, all the way to the border with the darkness. They were an illimitable number of them. Lucy shivered and wondered how long humanity could possible survive if they all got out. It seemed as if all the vampires in human history were assembled here.

None of the vampires saw her. She walked through their ranks in her borrowed pregnant body, listening to them all talk about what "good feeding Queen Jacqueline had promised," and how they were "impatient to start sinking their fangs into virgin throats." Others commented on how "humanity wouldn't know what had hit them."

Dressed as most of the bloodsuckers were in Renaissance/18th Century gear, the whole area around the castle had the atmosphere of an old country carnival to it.

The looks of starving bloodlust on the vampire's faces were such as to make a corpse shudder. Despite being wrapped in another woman's warm flesh, the ghost shivered.

Lucy steered Kate out of the dim ultraviolet and into the Darkness. Here there were many more vampires, and she was forced to listen to much more of their horrid bloodsucker conversation. All of it was of the same kind: how they would rip apart human necks, how they would drink and bathe in human blood. How they would make love in the gore of smeared human corpses. How they would desecrate churches and tear cowering priests to shreds.

Lucy walked Kate Nixon out of the Darkness and into the Madison House.

Once inside the house she realized she needed to be careful. There were demon guards inside the mansion; earlier she'd seen some patrolling its halls. *Remember the sentinels can see you!* She understood that the guards needn't be near the portal into the Darkness. They could be just about anywhere in the evil building.

I just need to be careful, she reassured herself. *I'm almost done. Just a little farther to go now and it'll be all over here.*

She walked Kate over towards the nearest staircase. She made the girl's fingers grip the bannister and take the first steps up. Kate's body was tiring from the unfamiliar exertion; Lucy could feel the strain in her muscles. But the body would make it upstairs and into the safe haven she'd prepared for it. Safe for now at least.

"Hey, stop—Princess Kate! What are you doing outside of your bedroom?" The voice was guttural with a sub-octave pitch. Human words formed by a throat ill designed for producing them.

Shit, Lucy thought. *The damn demon guards! And just when I was about finished here too.* She didn't look around. She just knew what was about happening now.

182

Concerned for her safety, as she was clearly walking in her sleep, the guards were going to politely escort her back into the Darkness and to her bedroom in the castle.

Shit. And I need this vampire bitch's baby for the cops to sacrifice to destroy this mansion forever.

Lucy heard the evil creatures' footsteps come closer to her. She knew she had only one chance of fooling them, but try as she might, she couldn't make either Kate's eyes or mouth open. There was clearly no way that she'd be able to tell the guards to leave her alone for the moment. And there was another danger. The guards' voices might bring out inquisitive vampires, who would in turn alert their queen that her security force were having a conversation with her sleepwalking daughter.

As fast as she could manage in Kate's pregnant body, Lucy began running up the stairs.

"Princess, wait."

She neither waited nor looked back. She kept running. Her only hope now was to lose her pursuers. She felt it just might be possible to give them the slip.

There was an angled turn in the stairway. Once she turned it, she could see back down the way she'd climbed. She saw the guards—two scaly, bulbous-eyed creatures that had no business whatsoever being on Earth—slowly climbing the lower half of the staircase after her. If they meant to ascend faster, then their immense size was slowing them down.

The pair of guards grunted with frustration as they followed her. They didn't hail her again. They'd clearly assumed the obvious: that the pregnant heiress to the vampire throne was walking in her sleep and had no idea what she was doing. If so, they'd missed an obvious question: why then was she fleeing from them?

Also, since they'd addressed Kate as 'Princess,' they clearly couldn't see the ghost inside her.

None of which really helped Lucy very much. She had to get away from them and fast at that. It looked as though she might make it, though her borrowed body was really tired now after its excursion, and its tiredness was seeping into her own mind, almost lulling her to sleep on the stairs.

She was, however, relieved at one advantage that the guards' silent pursuit gave her: no longer were they likely to attract the attention of any vampires.

Slowly—Kate was too tired to run now (wherever did one see pregnant women running anyway?)—Lucy reached the top of the stairs. She intended to go left, but then discovered she couldn't move.

She looked back. No, the guards hadn't grabbed her. The pair of guards were both now at the turn in the stairs, six or so feet below her. What had happened rather was that Kate's maternity dress had gotten snagged on a loose nail in the wooden bannister.

Panicking lest the guards reach them, Lucy bent the woman's body to free the dress. It wouldn't come free, so she began tugging on it.

The dress ripped free. Doing so, however, tripped Lucy/Kate up so she fell backwards. She landed heavily on her pregnant behind, with her legs jutting out over the top step. Kate's head jerked back slightly further and smacked against the corridor wall.

Seeing as she was 'riding along' inside an already unconscious woman, Lucy wasn't knocked out.

However, she was heavily disoriented, as though the shock of their body's landing had partly disconnected her from Kate.

The other thing the fall had done was break Kate's birth waters. Lucy felt the damp spillage trickle out of Kate's sex and pool under her buttocks.

The demon guards were both now past the turn in the stairs. In fact, Lucy realized, they were both almost touching her feet.

She rushed desperately to regain control over Kate's body. She did so, but not fast enough. The foremost of the two guards grabbed hold of her ankle. A soft grasp, not a violent one.

It happened then: One moment, the two guards were solicitously helping 'the royal vampire princess' to her feet, and the next moment...

Lucy didn't see too clearly how it began, but suddenly, both of the demon guards who'd been lifting her to her feet were stuck to the corridor walls and being sucked away into it.

Let go of by their hands, Lucy/Kate fell back to the corridor floor again. She sat there and watched the guards being sucked away into the walls.

The demons grunted in confusion and fought against the house. Their eyes bulged in horror. They stretched their hands towards her as if for help, but their resistance did them no good. In less than a minute after it began, it was over. They'd been completely absorbed into the building and the house walls looked normal again.

This house has to be stopped, Lucy thought in horror, *it's getting stronger and stronger. It's as bad as Jackie Nixon now. Eating people at will.*

185

She struggled to her feet and walked her borrowed body down the corridor, taking care to stay away from its walls.

A minute later, she pushed open a bedroom door and walked Kate over to its central bed. She lay Kate down in the bed.

Then, as slowly as she'd joined with the vampire, Lucy detached herself from her.

Once her ethereal self was again outside of Kate Nixon, Lucy felt extremely tired, as if *she'd* been the one walking out of the darkness, not her host body. Reviewing what had happened, she understood that her weakness was as a result of the glamor Kate was under. She realized too that the trance-spell was also the reason it had taken her so long to merge with Kate. Though not really advisable (for the host's sake), a union with an unenchanted person should happen much faster.

She looked at Kate again. The vampire bitch seemed unharmed; her breathing was normal. Kate's swollen belly twitched slightly, then twitched again. 'Baby on the way' signs for sure.

Lucy smiled coldly. It looked like the two policemen outside would soon have the little sacrifice they needed.

Grinning to herself at a job well done, the ghost vanished from the bedroom.

***

Sensing the child in the mother on the bed, the house was pleased. Soon, very soon, it would have what it wanted. Its power would be magnified by degrees. Already it could smell the unborn blood, smell its

186

strange misbalanced essence—for this child was both pure and evil: Pure for it had committed no sin it could be judged for; evil because of its tainted lineage. Even though Kate Nixon's and Will McConnellson's baby had been conceived before the mother's turning, growing it inside herself, feeding it from her own body had made it obscene before God.

Lucy's narrow escape on the stairway hadn't been accidental. Neither had it been coincidental. It had been the house's doing. The house had protected what it wanted. Sensing what was about happening, the corrupted mansion had eaten the guards, prevented them from returning the young mother to the realm of the undead. Even now, it still felt the psychic energy from the guards it had eaten.

A gentle breeze blew into the bedroom. The unconscious mother groaned in pain as her birth contractions began.

The house was delighted.

CHAPTER 25

Detectives Rich Vincent and Gary Bottles strode along the rear of the Madison House. At the moment, they were almost through laying out their explosive charges. Just a final pair to go.

All the ground floor lights inside were off, which gave them some confidence of not being discovered at their grim work. But not much. The house had a creepiness that they both felt. There was something distressingly unwholesome about it.

Without discussing it with one another, both Vincent and Bottles had the very strong impression that this goddamn house was the real vampire they were trying to stop. The trio of halogen floodlights affixed to the rear walls (and which brilliantly illuminated the yard) did little to lessen the feeling of dread the building gave them.

"I don't like it, whatever you say." Bottles said.

"Yeah, yeah," Vincent replied with irritation, though he was uncertain if Bottles was still talking about the proposed baby sacrifice or commenting on the horrible vibe the house was giving off. He suspected Bottles was talking about the house. From what the ghost Lucy had told them, this goddamn Madison mansion had swallowed up forty-plus people. If that didn't give one the creeps, what would?

He was hoping blowing this damn place up would free those missing people. But even Lucy couldn't guarantee that. Still, even if the already-missing weren't freed, destroying the mansion would prevent others from vanishing inside it.

Concerning the child sacrifice that Lucy said had to accompany the explosion to make it fully effective? Vincent intentionally wasn't thinking that far ahead. Best to take this shit one step at a time. Or else...or else, he'd be like Gary Bottles here, who at the moment couldn't see the woods for the trees. Damn, the way Bottles had been going on about 'the baby, the baby, the baby,' Vincent almost expected him to call the station and turn both of them in at any moment.

He looked over at Bottles now. "Hey, man, I don't like this criminal crap we're doing either, okay? But let's just get this over and done with. If we don't, from what Lucy told us, a whole lot more people will vanish and possibly die as well."

Stepping across a clump of flowers, he planted two final bundles of explosives under a half-open window. From a peek inside, this was a kitchen window. The packages were bulky and heavy and had to be handled with extreme care. (He and Bottles had each lugged one over from the car, same as for all the other drop points around the mansion.)

Once Vincent had set up the two packages, he stepped back and reviewed his blast calculations. This was the fourth group of explosive packages on this side. They'd planted similar amounts at strategic points all around the building. Sixteen places in all. Each side's explosives had enough power in themselves to level the mansion, but with all the steel reinforcement buildings had in them nowadays, one had to make properly sure.

He activated the detonator relay and ensured it was receiving on the right channel. You didn't want to hit the 'blow up' switch and wind up microwaving someone's chicken dinner for them.

Finally, he was convinced they were good to go.

He turned to face his partner. Vincent's main concern now was not being caught before they sent the building sky-high. And, not leaving any evidence that could be traced back to them. If anything went wrong here tonight, both he and Bottles were sure to be spending a long time in a stone motel. Fingerprints were never a problem in cases like this, but they needed to make sure they didn't drop anything personal that might get buried beneath the resulting rubble. One slip-up was all it took to ruin their lives and careers.

"I think we're about done here." He saw the look on Bottles' face but didn't comment. There wasn't anything new to say. Sure, sure, Bottles was pissed off that they were gonna have to butcher a little kid to get this over with. So? Did Bottles imagine that *he* liked the idea? The man must be nuts if he thought that.

Vincent understood his partner, though: the man had a family—a nice wife and kids—and right now, he was certain to be thinking of the first time he'd become a father—that wonderful moment when the doctor had handed him the kid with its tiny face all wrinkled up like a raisin, and he'd looked from it to his wife Barbara, who'd been exhausted but beaming with pleasure, and realized that they'd both just accomplished a miracle...

There wasn't any denying that it felt shitty to know that tonight, to finish this crazy thing, they were going to have to undo a similar miracle.

But still, from what Lucy had told them, doing that unthinkable deed was the only way they could stop the vampires. Vincent was convinced to the core of his bones that the ghost woman wasn't bullshitting them with her talk of vampires. They already had more than enough evidence that confirmed she was telling the truth. It was just that in a rational world, no one—not least of all he and his partner Bottles here—wanted to believe that evidence. It was the evidence of madness. But what about if you had the proof handed to you on a plate? What about when you *had to believe* the evidence? What then? What else could you do? Did you take what you knew was insane to your superiors; those who'd tag *you* as insane? Or did you act on it yourself and hope you could save the human race?

They'd made their choice. Vincent was certain it was the right one. Well, he hoped he wasn't just having an extra-vivid delusion that he'd wake up from tomorrow in a padded jacket.

Vincent crossed the flowerbed back to his partner's side. Together they began walking back toward the front of the house. At first neither man said a thing, both labored beneath the weight of their thoughts.

The silence didn't last long. This wasn't a night for silence.

"This sure is a crazy damn place," Bottles said before they'd taken ten steps.

191

"Huh?" Vincent asked. He'd been about making the same comment, but... well, he thought he'd just heard *something*.

"I was saying," Bottles repeated. "This place is crazy. It's almost making me believe this crap we're doing is the right thing."

"Shush," Vincent said. "Listen. Can you hear anything?"

Bottles got the urgency in Vincent's voice. Both men froze and waited, listening for hints that someone was aware of their presence.

"What are we supposed to be listening for?" Bottles asked after a short silence. This silent waiting was eating away at his nerves.

"I dunno. I just got the feeling we ain't alone out here."

"Lucy the child-snatching ghost again?"

Vincent ignored the jibe and nodded. "Could be, but it's not getting cold, is it? Both previous times she showed up, it felt like someone had just opened a freezer door."

"Yeah." Bottles looked up and along the side of the house, studying the stone walls and dark shimmering windows.

Vincent, meanwhile, ran his gaze over the yard's scattering of trees. He didn't, however, really expect someone to be watching them from behind the trees.

"Hey, Rich, was that third-floor light on when we came around the side of the house?"

Vincent looked up. "Yeah, I think so. It's only the ground floor windows that were all dark. What's the matter? You think someone might've been staring at us from up there? They'd have raised an alarm wouldn't they?"

"Yeah, Rich," I guess you're right."

Vincent forced a smile. "I guess I was wrong about hearing anything. Just a case of nerves. Let's head back to our car and wait for Lucy to show up with the kid."

"Aw, c'mon, man. You know I can't do this if the kid's involved. Rich, I got kids of my own. How'd you think I'd feel if someone kidnapped one of them?"

Vincent was about to blow up at Bottles. They'd been over this too many times already. To make an omelet, one needed to break eggs. In this case, the damn baby was the egg.

Still, he managed to control himself.

He tugged on Bottle's coat sleeve so that they both paused just before turning the corner of the house, right under one of the bright floodlights.

"Alright, man, we need to clear this up once and for all."

Bottles gazed at him sullenly. "Yeah? How?"

"Okay, man," Vincent said as calmly as he could manage. "If you don't want in on the human sacrifice angle, I'll handle that myself. I'll do it. You don't have to be involved at all. Just stay out of the way. Out of sight, they say, is out of mind." He stared intently at his partner, willing him to be calm and strong. "Are you with me?"

"But look, I'll know what we've done."

"What we'll have done is..." he paused for emphasis. "We'll have saved the damn entire human race. I for one, don't want to be goddamn vampire food."

"But..."

193

"Just listen, alright? Now, both to me and to you, the human race is way, way, way more important than some kid you've never met before."

"It's a baby. Its parents are gonna miss it."

"It might be an orphan. Look, forget that part, okay. Lucy said she'd get the baby. It's nothing to do with us where she gets it from. It might even be a vampire baby." He looked coldly at Bottles. "You got issues with doing in a vampire baby?"

"Yeah. A baby's a baby either way."

"Whatever. Like I said, just let me handle that shit. All I need from you is not to freak out on me and start having damn pangs of conscience after the deed has been done and turn us both in, 'cos you confessed to your damn wife Barb and that's what she says is the right fucking thing to do. You dig? Just assure me that that won't happen, and I'll take care of the rest."

"Hey, leave Barbara out of this."

"So long as you leave her out of it too. Remember, how you almost got us in trouble over the Jenkins's case 'cos Barb said she didn't like—"

Rich Vincent stopped speaking all of a sudden. This time there was no doubt about it. He'd heard something. A rough rustling sound, like feathers scraping the side of a window. Bottles was still staring belligerently at him like he wanted to engage him over his comments concerning his wife, but he ignored the man. Whatever was up there—his mind had suddenly cottoned onto the fact that the noise was coming from directly above them—was both unnatural and had no good intentions towards them either of them.

194

Even as he jerked out his service revolver and turned to stare up the side of the building, he could see it—whatever it was—hurtling down towards them. It was coming at a horrible speed. They were standing directly under the halogen lamp and, though angled away from them, its light was in Rich Vincent's eyes, not letting him see the onrushing thing clearly. Even so, he could tell that it was large, and black, and hairy, and had huge wings.

He fired at it. He got off a single shot, but it had already streaked past him.

Then he heard Bottles scream. He spun to face the man, ready to shoot, but what he saw was worse than what he'd expected.

Bottles stood there holding his neck, from which blood was gushing as though it was running from a tap. There were three deep slashes through Bottles' throat. He was desperately trying to cover them with his hands. The ground in front of him was already red with spilling blood.

"Shit!" Vincent gasped, as, gripping his throat, Bottles slowly sank to the stone walk.

The thing that had ripped out Bottles' throat now glared at Vincent. To his horror he clearly recognized Jackie Nixon's features in its hairy distorted face. It was this surprised recognition that prevented him from immediately shooting it.

The woman really is a goddamn vampire. The ghost wasn't bullshitting us! Dammit!

The vampire queen bared her teeth at him and he pissed himself, the urine running hot inside his right pants leg. So sharp! So long! The hound-like nose, the

195

ruby red eyes with their radiant insatiable hunger. The massive bat wings. The dark shaggy body!

With a snarl, Jackie Nixon stepped towards him.

Rich Vincent now unfroze and again tried to shoot the vampire-bat monster. But he'd left it too late. He did get his shots off, two of which he was certain hit the monster (as she grabbed him he saw a flare of pain in her eyes and felt her body jerk back) but then she had him.

Oh, God, NOOOO!!!

Her claws held him tight. His struggles against her grip were a total waste of time. She was too strong, the difference in their energies as vast as that between an adult athlete's and a toddler's.

He found it comical after that, how easily she bent his head to one side and sank her teeth into his neck. And then she was draining him of blood, fast and furious, while he stood there paralyzed, jerking from the pain and pissing himself again and wishing he'd listened to Bottles and left well enough alone, and that they'd both gotten the hell out of there while they still could. He tried screaming but all that came from his lips was a strangled croak.

After that, all he could do was wait to die.

To enable her to sink her teeth deeper into Vincent's neck, the vampire bent his head further to the left, till he found himself staring at Gary Bottles' corpse.

It was in this position that she drained him completely.

***

196

Delicious, Jackie Nixon thought, flinging the nosy policeman's corpse down on that of his partner. She stood by the pair of corpses and laughed at them.

Fools. Such damn fools they were to imagine they could take me on. I'm the vampire queen! You dumb humans will soon understand exactly what that means.

She kicked Detective Bottles' corpse and laughed loudly. Her laugh wasn't human, it was the satiated growl of a carnivore, the affirmative roar of a lioness fully sated on deer flesh.

The blood she'd drunk had greatly pacified her earlier anger on discovering that that stupid young priest William had survived her attempt to stamp him out like the pest that he was.

Indeed, the only reason Jackie had noticed the two men prowling her mansion was because she'd needed to let off steam.

Romeo Luiz was downstairs in the cellar studying in the *Grimoire Țepeș.* He was working on something new, he said, something that would both help their invasion, and put an end to that goddam pest William McConnelson. Romeo had even had the temerity to suggest that she was disturbing him with her endless pacing of the basement and her ceaseless impatient questioning as to the progress of his research. At another time she'd have punished him for his impertinence, but now, seeing the strain on his face, and thus deducing how serious he was, she'd left him to his studies.

He'd better hurry up though, she'd thought as she'd taken to the skies and floated over Melas, *we've only two hours left till midnight.*

197

She'd soared over the town with the predator's glint in her eyes, looking for a human morsel to snack on. She'd been frustrated to find none. Everyone had fled the town, scared shitless of her. Cowards, they all were. All humans were cowards.

But then, she'd grinned. Human cowardice would ensure her victory. This wasn't going to be like some *Dracula* movie, where there was one primary vampire with maybe a couple of wives, and a million brave humans out to stamp them out. No, tonight would be nothing like that. Nor would it be like the *Blade* or *Underworld* vampire series, where the undead though numerous and claiming dominance over the living, still did their best to avoid detection by those they fed on.

No. This time she had *thousands* of followers, and before tonight ended she'd have thousands more. And human blood would flow like wine down the throats of those who followed her.

And they will worship me forever and ever, she thought happily. *I, Jackie Nixon will be humanity's new God.*

It was with this megalomaniac satisfaction in her mind that she'd descended back down to the mansion to check on Romeo's progress.

And then she'd noticed the two skulking policemen. She imagined they were trying to break into the building. (Her vampire majesty had not witnessed Vincent and Bottles laying the explosive charges. She'd descended only after they'd done so, had first noticed them walking back to stand beneath the halogen lamp. As such, she had no idea what the two policemen had really come to her home to do.)

198

She absentmindedly kicked Bottles again, then stood with her wings flapping behind her, pondering a question.

She'd heard the two policemen discussing a baby. A woman named Lucy was supposed to bring them a baby. They'd also been ranting about stopping the vampires and— had Vincent said Lucy was going to bring them a 'vampire' baby? The vampire queen wasn't certain of that. The wind had blown loudly at that point and she'd not heard the actual words the cop had uttered. But she'd clearly heard them talking about a 'baby being delivered by someone named Lucy.'

Who is Lucy? And what do the cops want with a baby anyway?

At first, she was troubled, but then she relaxed, with a wide smile on her feral face. She already had one baby soon to be born. Having an additional infant being delivered to her doorstep couldn't hurt any. She just needed to be on hand when 'Lucy,' whoever she was— it was most likely a codename—brought the baby here to hand it to the two policemen. Lucy herself would provide a little snack before she took on the world.

With those pleasant thoughts in mind, vampire queen Jackie Nixon bared her teeth at the moon. She licked her bloody lips. After a last look at the two fresh human corpses by her feet, she flapped her immense black wings and took to the sky again, off to reenter the mansion by the top-floor window from which she'd departed it.

Time to go find out what Romeo's big discovery is, she thought a little dreamily. Then her eyes turned cold. *That warlock son-of-a-bitch had better not have been*

199

wasting my time! Royal paramour or not, any more goddamn setbacks in my plan of conquest and I'll rip his head off for sure.

CHAPTER 26

Almost at the Madison House, William and Jay Cristiano heard the first gunshot from up ahead. William instantly swerved the RAM pickup truck under some roadside trees and cut the engine.

"Trouble up ahead," Jay said.

"Someone's shooting the vampires."

William had finished saying this when there were two more shots. Then silence.

They waited a while, but there were no more gunshots. William looked at Jay. "What do you think?"

Jay thought, the scars on his face creasing into ridges and furrows. "That house is full of vampires, right?"

"Yeah, so?"

"And we both know that vampires can't be killed with bullets, right?"

"Yeah?"

"So, I think what we just heard was someone trying not to become a vampire's dinner."

"In which case," William added, "the fact that we haven't heard a gunshot since then clearly means that the victim's attempt to defend themselves was a waste of time and they now reside in the belly of the beast anyway."

"Quite an astute observation, Father McConnellson," Jay Cristiano said. "Most definitely right."

"So, what do we do now?"

Jay shrugged. "We wait a bit. No point rushing into an ambush."

They sat in the parked car and waited.

CHAPTER 27

Looking up from the *Grimoire Țepeș*, Romeo Luiz smiled at Jackie, "I can report success, your majesty. I've figured everything out."

"Wonderful," she replied. He'd bowed while speaking, but the act had struck her as more insubordinate that if he'd remained upright. She studied his face to see if it held any traces of mockery. She couldn't tell.

For once, however, Romeo seemed certain of himself. That was good. They no longer had time for dilly-dallying.

They were not alone in the candle-lit cellar. Several of the higher ranking resurrected—both male and female—lounged about following the proceedings with interest. Jackie studied their undead faces. All had the same expression of reverence for her mingled with eagerness to leave the confines of the Darkness and feed. Empty bellies; hungry eyes.

She returned her attention Romeo. She nodded impatiently at him. "Alright, tell me. What have you discovered?"

He looked around. "Not here. Come with me."

He stood up and touched her arm. She felt an electric shock as he touched her and then felt a rush of demonic wind as Romeo's magic spell whisked them both away from the cellar.

"Where are we going?" she gasped. But there was no need for him to reply. They'd already arrived at their destination. They were once again out in the Darkness, out on the cliff that faced the lair of the Red Beast of Hell.

A cold wind whipped in from the sea, chilling Jackie, and she instinctively drew closer to Romeo. He put an arm around her. It was better when she was like this, he felt. Her endless royal bitching had been getting on his nerves. True, one obeyed a vampire queen without question—that was the law—but a queen was supposed to show some concern for her subjects'—and lover's feelings. Being royal was more than just bossing everyone around as if they were employees in one of her companies.

"Why have you brought us here?" Jackie asked.

Romeo pointed across a vast lake to the humongous stone concealing the lair where the Red Beast slept its eternal slumber. "We will need our sleeping friend after all, your majesty."

She shivered involuntarily. The very thought of the Red Beast filled her with an instinctive dread. The beast was a thing of horror, a horror even she was unwilling to face. "But you said we wouldn't need it anymore."

He looked down at her and grimaced. "At that point I had no idea young Mister McConnellson was still alive. Nor did you."

"And how does the Red Beast help us with that. Do you intend on having it kill him?"

Romeo shook his head. "No."

"What then?"

"I intend to use the beast as a diversion."

She frowned at him. "A diversion? Can you stop being so cryptic and just explain what you mean?" She stared down at the black water below and felt centuries of death and horror reflected back at them from its murky depths. Queen or not, this part of her realm filled her with unease. "Romeo," she prompted him. "Go on for—" she'd been about saying "for heaven's sake," but with a laugh realized that would be utterly inappropriate here. Completely inappropriate with one of Hell's prime horrors lurking just across the way. "Just go on. The damn suspense is pissing me off."

"Alright, darling. First of all, permit me to review our plan so far."

"Yes, alright, but do it quickly."

Realizing that some of his lover's previous bad temper seemed to be returning and that if he didn't calm it, she'd soon begin treating him like her hired help again, Romeo quickly went on:

"At twelve tonight, two-and-a-half hours from now, we enter the human world. However, the young priest and his—um, helper—may be waiting for us out there. And I've no way of telling what the pair of them have planned. My greatest concern is—"

She pulled away and stared coldly at him. "Sometimes, Romeo, I don't understand you. As powerful a warlock as you are, you seem scared stiff of this child William. So he's a damn priest, so damn what? We'll stamp him out like a roach. Sometimes you're so wishy-washy, I regret that we share the same bed."

205

His eyes clouded over at the rebuke, then he smiled. His smile was even colder than hers, colder that the chill of Darkness that wrapped them both. "You seem to have very quickly forgotten what happened the last time you tried to stamp him out."

He waited for her retort, but it didn't come—those deaths, particularly the deaths of all the Belladonna Rose band members had shaken them both. In his case, because the band had been like family to him. In her case, because their inglorious passing had reminded her of her own mortality. A goddess she might be; but she was a goddess that could be killed.

"Yes," he chided her gently, "you—all of us in fact— are immortal, but we're not invulnerable. Given the right conditions—one of which is our underestimating what he's capable off—that damn 'child' as you so dismissively keep referring to him, can upset your entire kingdom, pull your rug of royalty out from under your feet and upend you into..." He gestured down into the sea. "So, I advise caution."

"But, but..." She disliked him speaking to her like she was a child, but she disliked even more the notion that her plans of human conquest and dominion could crumble because of one insignificant member of the species. "But... but..."

Romeo sensed her confusion and worked to enlighten her. "In himself, William McConellson, is an insignificant gnat. Compared to the noble vampire race, the priest is less than an ant; a grub you could grind to a pulp with the heel of your shoe. The problem is what the young man represents. As I said, he's a 'Chosen One,' a person powered by the *other side* to oppose our forces

206

of darkness. Good to counter our evil. As such, even at his weakest, he can hurt us. When he is strong—and I sense this in him now—he is deadly."

"What is to be done then? Look, Romeo, just stop the suspense nonsense and tell me!"

"We'll use the distraction I mentioned. We'll sic the Red Beast of Hell on him." He frowned. "Now, don't misunderstand me: The red beast is too appalling a creature to let loose untamed. If we let it out into the human world, it will create devastation even we can't control. But... the spell I was researching was one to weaken it."

"Weaken it? Can it be weakened?"

"Yes, to a point..." he paused in thought, not exactly sure if he understood the consequences of such a scheme, but nevertheless resumed confidently: "We'll need your grandson's blood again, I'm afraid."

"Please go ahead. The child's a damn half-breed. He's a disgrace to me even before he's born. Besides we'd already planned to sacrifice him before discovering it wasn't necessary anymore, so his death is no real loss. My daughter can always have another kid."

The vampire queen was pleased. Since Victor's death, she'd imagined any number of catastrophes which might befall her reign and her plans. In the event of any of those disasters occurring, she'd imagined she'd be left stranded at sea without the Elder Vampire's counsel, however grudgingly given. But now, she realized she needn't have worried; Romeo was proving more than adequate, though he was very indecisive at times and needed constant prodding and prompting to kick start his creativity.

"So," Romeo went on, pleased that her majesty appeared to agree with him, "maybe a half-hour or so before we launch our attack on humanity, we'll let the Red Beast of Hell out of its ageless captivity. We'll let it out of the mansion—there's a spell to transport it directly outside your house—and let it find William and his helper. Or they'll find it. They're both certain to be outside the mansion right now."

"I didn't notice them while I was out flying. The only persons I saw were those two policemen from a couple days ago."

Romeo Luiz's eyes narrowed at that information. "Oh? What were they doing?"

She bared her fangs at him. "Providing dinner for me, of course. The taller cop was particularly delicious. You know how much I love mature blood-wine."

They both laughed at her joke, then Romeo went on: "So, where was I?"

"You were telling me how the priest and his friend should be hanging around outside the mansion by now."

"Yes, yes, that I was. So, we set the Red Beast against William the priest and leave them to fight it out. The beast may be weak enough for William to subdue, but not immediately. While they battle with it, we'll all sneak out of the house and spread out over the countryside."

"I dislike this 'sneaking' bit. A queen leading an invasion should be bold. "

"It's a military maneuver, darling. Discretion is considered the better part of valor."

She nodded and straightened her hair with her fingers. Across the dark water the black rock waited with its promise of total victory for her forces. "Alright, I'll go along with the cowardly *sneaking out* strategy. And while we're *sneaking out,* William and his friend will be distracted, right? But... but what if they ignore the Red Beast and try to stop us regardless?"

"The Red Beast of Hell isn't something one *can* ignore, your majesty. It's so horrible it arrests the attention. Besides, it'll be trying to kill them. They'll have no choice but to fight with it."

"But what if they can't subdue it?"

"If they can't then the priest won't really be the Chosen One, will he?" Romeo smiled. "It's a win-win situation for us either way. If the red beast kills them, then we don't have to worry about either of them again. If, however, as I expect to happen, the damn priest and his partner force it back into its ageless slumber, all we need do then is hunt the pair of them down at our leisure once the world's ours."

He saw she was musing on this and added: "Yes, and there's one more little detail about our vampire invasion that I need to clarify with you. A very important detail."

"Yes—what's that?"

"Well, remember that originally our troops were supposed to begin attacking the nearby towns, and from there spread further across the state and outwards?"

"Yes? So what's the change?"

"In light of new developments, I think we should start all the attacks outside of the state. In Ohio, Maryland, and Pennsylvania. We don't work in West Virginia tonight at all."

"I don't understand why such needs to be the case. If we begin closer to home, we turn more people more quickly. The more our numbers are, the more unstoppable we become and the faster too."

"Oh, it's just an additional precaution, that's all, in case our little priest has more divine help about to turn up."

"Divine?" Now Jackie's face creased up in a frown. "He's got *divine* help? Romeo, what the hell is all this?"

Romeo shrugged. "It's very complicated. But forget it for the moment."

"How can I?"

"That's why this new strategy is perfect for us." With both hands, he made an expansive gesture out over the black waters. "Now, please, permit me to liken our invasion plans to the spread of an infectious disease. At its source, the outbreak can easily be contained by one or two doctors. The further, however, that the illness spreads from where it originated—the more doctors one needs." He grinned coldly. "Only in this case, there aren't any others, see? The only two anti-vampire physicians available will be busy fighting the Red Beast. And when they're done subduing it, because we launched our invasion outside of the state, they'll have no idea where we are. And by the time they find out, we'll be literally everywhere, in every state of the federation. And there may be a hundred thousand of us then." He made a violent crushing gesture with his fist. "Enough to wipe them both out for good."

"I love it. It's a genius plan! Vampire queen Jackie Nixon couldn't help herself. She leapt on Romeo Luiz and kissed him hard. She was delighted. She saw no way this plan could possibly go wrong.

CHAPTER 28

In the upstairs mansion bedroom where Lucy Westerna had left her, pregnant Kate Nixon was finally giving birth.

The mother-to-be was covered in cold sweat. It had soaked through her dress and soaked the bed sheets.

Unconscious and unattended by a midwife, her body did all the work. Kate herself felt nice and warm, floating in a cocoon of fluffy cotton. She was aware of very little, her only impression of the world around came through dreams. Most of her dreams were nightmares in which a woman with a familiar face and long teeth was killing a little child.

In a short while, her birth canal distended, and her child slid headfirst out into the world. The baby boy forced her lax thighs apart with its bloody exit. There was the pause of a few seconds and then he began yelling for food.

Somehow, the newborn's cries penetrated the spell of slumber that bound its mother. Unable to move and feed it, Kate Nixon nonetheless smiled in her magical dream that never ended. It was pleasant change from her nightmares. At least this particular child was alive and safe where the fanged woman could not harm it.

211

CHAPTER 29

The ghostly Lucy Westerna was sitting by the gateway to the Darkness when she heard the cry of the newborn child. Lucy had been watching the portal for the emergence of a search party looking for the missing vampire princess.

"Oh no, I got carried away," she muttered worriedly, kicking an imaginary stone. She felt alarmed now; someone might hear the child's shrieks.

With a look of deep concern on her face, she vanished from the portal hall. A moment later, she was upstairs in Kate's bedroom. Yes, the vampire's child was born and bawling its damn eyes out.

She studied the crying infant for a moment.

"Hey," she told it, "you look like you'd grow up to be quite handsome. Past tense since I don't intend letting that happen."

The newborn boy had stopped crying on hearing her voice. She bent over it and felt sad. Sad because this child would never have an adult life. Despite her anger against the baby's mother and grandmother, she had no real desire to kill the child. She was a woman herself and felt like mothering it instead. But at the same time as her maternal instinct kicked in, she felt *the house* again. She was constantly conscious of the house's growing evil,

212

but now, she recognized that something about that very evil had changed.

If the building was human, she'd have said it was *happy*. Happy at this child's birth.

She shuddered, suddenly understanding: *It wants this baby for itself. It wants to feed on it and grow stronger.*

She stared down at the little boy. The child was looking up at her. It looked perplexed. Where was its food?

She smiled at it. "You're about going on a long trip. You might as well do so on a full belly."

It was at times like this that the actual restrictions of being dead—i.e. not being able to grip objects with one's hands—annoyed her.

Still, she did what she could. With intense concentration, she gripped the child with her mind and slid it up over its mother's body. Additional concentration positioned the boy with his mouth over Kate's left breast. She'd draped him with his stubby torso across Kate's right breast, so he'd not fall off. A little more mental concentration ripped Kate's dress apart and put her left nipple in her son's mouth. One more burst of concentration flew two pillows across to Kate's sides, bracing the infant in place, so he'd not slip out of position.

Lucy stood back and reviewed her mindwork.

The little boy was suckling lustily away, all well for the moment in his little world. Lucy thought he looked funny draped like that, with his uncut umbilical cord running out between his legs like a tail. But it could not be helped at the moment. Kate's placenta was out of her

213

body now. Lucy nodded dully at the red mess between Kate's legs, then she teleported herself out of the bedroom, downstairs to look for the two policemen.

"Noooooo!" she screamed a moment later, on finding Detectives Rich Vincent's and Gary Bottles' corpses. "NOOOOOOOOO!!!"

She stood and gaped at the two dead men, the harsh sentences of their deaths made even harsher by the way the white halogen lighting illuminated their bodies. Both cops had horrified expressions on their faces. Bottles was covered in blood, blood that formed a pool around his head, blood spilled from his slashed throat. In stark contrast, Rich's corpse was bloodless, completely exsanguinated, with those two horrible telltale punctures in its neck.

This is Jackie Nixon's work, Lucy immediately knew. It felt to her as if the vampire queen had left a psychic stamp on both corpses. *It can't have been anyone else except that evil witch.*

An incredible feeling of depression suddenly descended on Lucy. The sense of complete and final defeat. *Oh, it's finished,* she thought with heartfelt horror. *Humanity is finished! The vampires have won!*

The ghost began weeping, cold ethereal tears spilling down her face.

214

CHAPTER 30

"She's what!?" Jackie Nixon asked Romeo Luiz. She wasn't sure she'd heard him clearly. "Kate is what!?"

The warlock held the princess's bedroom door open for his queen. She peeked in, then whirled on him, grabbing hold of his wizard's robes and yelling in his face: "Romeo, tell me, where the hell is she!?"

He didn't reply her for almost a minute, his face as cold and impassive as the eternal night visible outside the princess's bedroom window with its violently fluttering drapes. All that while Jackie clung to him as if to let him go would be to let go of her hopes of world dominion. She felt a incipient dread creeping up on her, like a beast stalking her. It seemed impossible that so many obstacles could be put in her way, each on the heels of the other: First, needing to kill that traitor Victor to let her hordes out into the world; then the fiasco when she'd sent those same hordes off to dispose of that silly priest; then the two cops investigating her; and now?—this most ridiculous of all hindrances to her vampire takeover plans.

Kate was missing. Missing? How the hell...

"How in the hell can she be missing?" Jackie whimpered at her warlock lover. "Give me an answer,

215

dammit! I need an answer right now!" Her voice was desperate.

"There isn't a whole lot of mystery over what happened, darling," Romeo finally replied her.

She let go of him and stepped back. "So tell me, where is she?"

"She's been kidnapped."

"Kidnapped you say?"

He pulled her into the empty bedroom and shut the door behind them. Jackie sat on her missing daughter's vacant bed; Romeo stood facing her. "It's the only logical explanation. Your daughter was unconscious. She couldn't have left by herself; which means someone else stole her away."

"Who? Another traitor?"

"No." He crossed the room to lean against the bedroom door. "It's not one of our own people; we can be a hundred percent certain of that. The vampires all worship you as queen. Also, Victor, the only one who disputed your claim to the vampire throne, is dead now."

She mused on this, curiosity and anger now replacing the worry on her face. "So who can have done this then?"

"We'll find out," he said.

"We don't have much time!" she spat at him, her face now feral again. Already, a rage was building in her, a fierce anger that anyone would dare trifle with her or attempt to thwart her ambitions this close to their fruition. "We've at most an-hour-and-a-half left!"

Romeo smiled back at her, though he clearly wasn't amused either. He pulled open the bedroom door and gestured out into the corridor. "In that case, your majesty, I suggest that we use the little time we've got wisely."

She walked past him out of the bedroom. "I wonder why the damn guards weren't *guarding!*" she growled. "Now look what's it's caused."

"A minor oversight," Romeo said, as together they strode down the corridor. "No one could have predicted this would happen." He scratched his chin. "Still, yes, there's the possibility that one of the sentinels might have noticed something. We'll question them first."

"Forget it!" Jackie snapped. "They're not fools. If any of them had seen Kate being borne off, they'd have raised the alarm."

Nodding, Romeo pulled her to a halt with a tug on her sleeve. "You're right, your majesty. In that case, we'd better return to the human world. I propose to hold a spirit consultation in the demonic cellar. I've a crystal ball there that we'll use."

"Yes! Let's go quickly!"

He took her hand again and spirited them back to the cellar.

***

"I don't believe this," Romeo said, looking up from peering into his crystal ball. "I can sense that she's close, but..." he gestured at the ball, "you can see for yourself how cloudy it is." He was seated on a high stool, with the ball precisely positioned in front of him.

"What does this mean?" Jackie asked impatiently. She couldn't stand this. It seemed to her as if Romeo had again reverted to his previous incompetence. "Dammit,

Romeo, what is all this nonsense? One minute, you've a solution to our problems, then the next minute you're acting like—like I don't even know what to liken you to! Maybe some magician's novice apprentice. For hell's sake, man, get your damn act together!"

He was clearly controlling his anger when he sullenly replied, "What it means, *darling*, is that something is *blocking* the damn signal. Think of the damn ball like a television. If something—" he left off the statement, too angry to continue.

She realized she'd angered him. That wouldn't do; silly man or not, she needed him. Besides necromancy and her scholarly studies with her father Walter, this advanced magic was well over her head, but one did need it. She wished she wasn't so reliant on Romeo Luiz, but what was it they said about wishes and horses?

She relented in her rage and bent over him. "I'm sorry, darling," she whispered in his ear so the vampire lords and ladies in the room wouldn't hear her apology. "I'm under so much stress today, it's almost driving me mad. Whoever thought that being a queen would be so much of a headache, huh? All you ever see them do on TV is eat cake and order people heads to be chopped off."

He laughed, then whispered back. "You're forgiven, darling. Now, order the lords in the room here to give orders to the rank and file to immediately start searching the Darkness for your daughter. It'll give everyone something to do."

Jackie instantly turned and barked out the order. The lords, all previously as immobile as painted statues, hurried from the room. Soon the only vampires present

218

with Jackie and Romeo were Jackie's four ladies-in-waiting, four gaunt noblewomen in sparkling long evening dresses and tight corsets who sat as motionless as their male companions had; most likely because they were yet to recover fully from their millennia-long blood-lack. The four women had apparently been ladies-in-waiting to the last vampire leader, and were now simply reprising their previous court positions for their new ruler. Once given the opportunity, they would get to work, pampering and catering to every whim and caprice of the new queen.

Ignoring the four noblewomen, Jackie asked Romeo, "And us, what do we do now while everyone else is searching everywhere?"

"We try to figure out what is blocking my finding out where Kate is." He tapped the crystal ball, its murky contents shifting like storm clouds at the strike of his fingers.

"Hmmm!" Jackie pulled up a stool and sat beside him. "Could it be this mansion blocking your locating her?"

"This mansion?" Romeo replied her, with a touch of disquiet. "What makes you think that?"

***

It *was* the Madison mansion blocking Romeo Luiz's attempts to locate Kate. Now that the child was born, the building was beside itself with glee. Like a thirsty dog, it lapped up the energy it felt radiating from the little boy. While the babe suckled on its mother's breasts, the building in turn suckled on the child's tainted aura. Then

219

it rested in satiation, basking in impressions of the glory to come.

Its malevolent mind now began pondering the problem of how to topple the child off its mother's body and onto the floor, so it could absorb the little boy and all his energies. Either that or a way to bring the child sideways to touch one of its walls.

(At this point, just like the ghostly Lucy who'd left the bedroom a short while earlier, the Madison mansion also felt the frustration being sentient but lacking hands.)

The child suckled then fell asleep. Propped up on one breast, hemmed in by pillows, its tiny infant snores pleased the room immensely.

Soon, my child soon, we will be one. And then...

In the meantime, however, the building jealously threw up a paranormal barrier around Kate's bedroom. This barrier was to prevent Lucy's return. The house had sensed that the ghost woman wanted the baby for her own uses. It didn't know what her purposes were, but it knew they involved removing the little boy from his mother, and from it—the house's—ambit. That was completely unacceptable. The Madison House would not permit such to happen.

That being the case it defended itself, supernaturally 'locking' the new mother's bedroom so the ghost would be unable to re-enter it; at least not before it had consumed the baby. Afterwards didn't matter.

Unfortunately for Jackie Nixon and Romeo Luiz, the mansion's blocking off the ethereal Lucy Westerna also completely neutralized every spell Romeo cast to locate Kate from penetrating her bedroom's walls.

***

"The house?" Romeo Luiz asked again.

"Well, it is a possibility," Jackie said. "Remember all the effort that went into building this damn place. It might have decided to go into business for itself."

Romeo mused on this, then shook his head. "No, my darling queen, I must disagree with you on this one. For this building to be responsible..." His brow creased up in thought. "Well, it would have to be alive, wouldn't it?"

She didn't immediately reply. Instead, she leapt down off her stool, walked over to the nearest wall and pressed her hand against it. She kept the hand there, so Romeo could see how the not-quite-stone/not-quite-flesh surface pulsed against it.

"Alive, huh? Whatever the hell do you call this?"

"I believe he means, your majesty," one of her ladies-in-waiting replied her, "that the building would need to be able to *think*."

Romeo cast a grateful smile at the noblewoman. She smiled back, baring her fangs at him. She had a generous bosom, and a hunger in her eyes that was clearly more than just the desire to sink her neck into some hapless throat. She winked at him. Romeo quickly looked away. Hell no. The woman must be crazy to even think that. Jackie would never tolerate that nonsense from either of them.

"Oh." Jackie pulled her hand off the rapidly throbbing surface. "No, even I find the concept of intelligent houses too far-fetched to believe in." She snapped her fingers at Romeo. "Okay, man, get on with it. We've no time to waste. Try another goddam spell!'' She calmed a little (she'd not missed the subtle exchange of glances between her lady-in-waiting and her warlock), then sweetly added: "Please, darling, you know our success tonight depends entirely on you."

His ego massaged, Romeo smiled. "Of course, your majesty. At once."

With an unnecessary flourish for ladies' benefit, he opened the *Grimoire Țepeș* to a fresh page. He slit his wrist with a knife, let a few drops of his blood drip onto the clouded crystal ball, then began intoning deeply in a guttural drone:

Around him, the queen and her women licked their lips as the delightful smell of Romeo's shed blood filled their nostrils. Its wonderful scent built their anticipation of tonight's human slaughter to a fever pitch.

CHAPTER 31

Finally, William and Jay Cristiano arrived at the Madison House.

The gates, which Jackie Nixon had installed at the end of Raccoon Run Road where the driveway ended in a cul-de-sac just below the mansion, were wide open. William drove on through.

The yard was brightly lit by three banks of halogen lamps. They parked their explosive-laden truck in the shadows beneath a large oak tree and got out.

In the interim since hearing the gunshots, they'd rigged the explosives to blow. Well, Jay Cristiano had. William had watched him wire the explosives in the truck bed together, connecting blasting caps and detonators, then wrapping fifty or so feet of detcord around it all.

When they'd climbed back into the front of the vehicle afterwards, William had the impression that Jay had just turned the RAM pickup truck into a bomb.

"Man, what is this?" William asked worriedly. "Are we on some kind of a suicide mission now? We're gonna drive into the mansion and blow it up along with ourselves?"

Jay's scarred face had creased into a cold smile. He'd looked skywards. "Let's just say, the Lord works in mysterious ways; his wonders to perform."

"Man, you already said that earlier. What are you getting at?"

"It's a mystery."

William had let it go. He'd concentrated on sitting as still as a scared mouse. He gripped his cross and told a rosary or two. He'd had the sinking feeling that wired up like Jay had it now, if their truck even hit a speed bump, they'd both be meeting God in person. And where would the world be then?

Now, Jay pointed at the mansion. "The building has grown even more powerful since you were last here, William. I doubt even the vampires understand what they've set in motion."

William nodded. He could *feel* what Jay meant. Staring at the building gave him the creeps—maybe because he knew what had gone into erecting it—all those mingled ashes and the soul stones, all those disquieted psyches now trapped inside it. He simply wanted to bomb the mansion to hell and be done with it. Really, that should have been simple enough; just blow the damned building up and drive off into the sunset like a Catholic hero.

However, there was a complication. "I've got to reenter the Darkness and find Kate," he said. "I can't let the portal close knowing she's trapped in there and knowing what her mother has planned for her."

Jay looked at his watch. "Not yet though. The vampires may be expecting us. We'll enter the house in a little while. But for now, let's keep a watch out here."

So they watched from behind the oak.

***

The house sensed the priest on its grounds. He was Good and it was Evil. It hated him. In addition, it hated even more the priest's companion. In a paroxysm of rage, the mansion focused all its attention on the pair. It wanted to drive them away; to make them flee from its presence.

After gathering up what it felt was a sufficient charge of negative energy, it projected this energy as a dark wind at the intruders, flung it across the yard at them.

***

All of a sudden a gale had arisen in the front yard.

"Hey, what the he—" William remembered he was consecrated again and managed not to swear. "I mean, what in God's name is this?"

The wind was whipping the leaves of the trees everywhere. The force of the wind was even ripping branches off of trees and flinging them about. Swirling leaves, acorns, and twigs filled the air. One or two smaller trees bent as if they would tear themselves out of the ground. Tellingly, it was only the trees on their side, the right side of the yard, that were thus affected. The left side the yard was entirely free of the violent winds.

"It's the house," Jay said placidly, making the sign of the cross at the building. "It senses us and wants

225

nothing to do with us." Then to William's surprise, he strode forward into the gale and yelled, "Peace, Be Still!!!" at it.

The gale immediately calmed. The trees stop shaking. The swirling leaves fluttered to the ground.

"Now I've seen everything," William thought. Squinting, he could see the force that had caused the violent wind visibly retreating back toward the building. He could see a distortion of the air that shrunk rearward a foot at a time. The distortion hit the stone frontage and vanished inside it. The house seemed to tremble.

Jay walked back under the oak and they resumed their wait.

***

The house was defeated but not cowed. It felt it simply had not been forceful enough. It rallied itself for another attack on the 'Good' intruders. It didn't want them anywhere inside it, and it knew they intended to enter it. This time it determined to HURT the pair; to wound, and if possible, kill them.

This time it pooled all its available strength for its attack, including that it was using as a shield around Kate Nixon's room. There was no danger of its precious baby being stolen: at the moment the ghost, after repeated failed attempts to project herself past its paranormal barricade, had retreated downstairs to the hall that housed the portal to the undead realm. The ghost was both frustrated and confused. The house was satisfied that for the moment it had discouraged her from trying to reach the baby again.

226

It sucked up as much dark force as it could drain out of itself, and in a concentrated blast, flung this at the hated human enemies. This time it would harm them for sure.

The blast streaked across the yard towards the tree the pair hid behind.

***

At that very moment, down in the basement of the mansion, Romeo Luiz's crystal ball cleared and he saw clearly.

"Jackie, quick! We're through!" he called to his mistress.

She, who'd been glumly studying one of Romeo's magic books with disinterest while he ticked off spell after spell that didn't work, quickly looked into the crystal ball.

"Yes, there's my little Sleeping Beauty," the vampire queen said nastily. She quickly also noted the baby sleeping on her daughter's chest. "Oh, and she's given birth to our sacrifice too." She stamped her foot. "But, where the hell is she, Romeo? That's what we need to find out." Can't you tune this thing any better? At the moment it's just showing the pair of them and the bed. Can you zoom it out a little? Then I might recognize the location."

"Of course, your majesty" Romeo said. He waved his hand over the crystal ball to meet her request; but at that moment three things happened:

First, all the candles in the cellar winked out.

227

Second, the interior of Romeo's crystal ball turned milky and confused again.

Third, they felt a massive shock hit the building as if a bomb had gone off. The shock flung all the ladies-in-waiting off their seats and sent them sprawling across the room. Ditto for their mistress, who was caught by Romeo just before she would have smashed her fangs against the stone altar.

"What the hell was that?" Jackie Nixon asked. It sounded like a bomb just went off somewhere

"Not a bomb," Romeo Luiz corrected her with a worried expression his face. "That was a massive injection of paranormal energy into the building. Something just hit the house with—" Romeo stopped speaking and cocked an ear like he'd just heard something.

"Paranormal energy? What do you mean—?" Then she too heard what Romeo had.

It was a baby's wail. Though thin and ephemeral, like a shriek in a badly dubbed movie, there was no mistaking what it was.

The infant's wail came again. This time they heard it clearly. The noise was coming from directly overhead, somehow filtering down through the layers of stone.

Jackie's four ladies-in-waiting had now all picked themselves up off the floor. One of them pointed up. "The child is clearly in the mansion, your majesty."

Jackie smiled. It was a cold and evil smile. She extended a hand to Romeo. "Let's go, Romeo," she said. "My grandson sounds rather lonely. I think it's time for him to meet his grandmother, don't you?"

***

The house stopped shaking. This time it *was* cowed. The two people it had tried to destroy were both still alive. The scarred one had done something—spoken yet another command—and all the force it had hurled at the pair had rebounded back at it. The energy it had cast at them had streaked violently back inside itself, making it feel like it was caught inside an earthquake. The building wasn't flesh and blood; as such it couldn't feel pain, but it felt a form of shame at being defeated. And there was no question about its defeat. It had no 'heart' for a continuation of the contest, at least not at the present time.

Now it did the only thing it could; the only thing it considered paramount and utterly necessary. It restored its paranormal shield over the room with the baby.

***

Wow, that was something else, William thought in awe as burnt oak leaves rained down over him. *Definitely something else.*

When the house had cast that beam of force at them, William had thought he and Jay were both goners, for sure. But Jay had once again stepped out and called something into the oncoming red blast of light. William hadn't heard what he'd said, but a transparent force field had appeared out of nowhere and blocked off the house's attack.

229

He'd watched the red light. It looked like some kind of 'slow' laser beam—it moved in the same way that the lightsaber blades came gradually out of their handles in the Star Wars flicks. The beam had hit the force field and bounced back across the yard at the mansion. When it hit the mansion, the building had shook and rumbled and finally settled again.

The force field had vanished immediately after protecting them both. Jay, however, was still standing out there watching the house, in case it had any more tricks up its sleeve.

More incinerated leaves rained down on William. A 'splinter' of the house's flung energy had leapt over the force field and hit the oak tree. There had been no flash of flame or sight of fire; the tree had simply instantly withered. At the moment, it was no better than ash. Personally, William couldn't even quantify how relieved he was that the force beam hadn't missed the tree and instead hit their truckload of explosives.

Jay Cristiano checked his wristwatch then walked back under the tree. "I think it's about time to get inside there."

William nodded. "Yeah, sure. I daresay the house won't be messing us with for a while, right?"

CHAPTER 32

Flanked on either side by a demon guard, Jackie Nixon and Romeo Luiz emerged from the mansion cellar into the main house.

"This is the sort of time when you wish cellphones worked in the Darkness," Jackie spat as their party of four strode across the tiled floor, past the portal that led to their realm of evil.

Romeo didn't reply. He felt exactly the same. The route to the Darkness lay open, a jagged rent in reality. It was also completely deserted now, all the vampires having departed into their realm and scattered everywhere to look for Kate. With it being impossible to 'phone home' as it were, the vampire queen had dispatched her four ladies-in-waiting into the Darkness, ordering them to hurry and round up everyone, telling them the royal princess had been found. The vampires were to return to the portal at once to await the strike of midnight.

They paused in the middle of the hallway, the gateway to the vampire realm a black hole behind them.

"So we know she's in the mansion," Romeo said. "And we know she's in a bedroom, but which bedroom exactly?" After the mansion's strange quaking ceased,

231

the crystal ball had again refused to show anything but a milky obscurity.

"We'll search all of them," Jackie retorted. "It won't take long. The mansion has sixteen bedrooms: four on this ground floor for the servants, and six on each of the two upper floors. She wasn't in *my* bedroom—I could tell that at a glance: the bed was too small—but she could be in just about any of the others."

"We've an hour till midnight," Romeo said.

"It'll be enough, I should think." Jackie headed for the stairs. She turned to their giant companions. "You two, search the servants' bedrooms. Hurry it up; break the damn doors down if they're locked. If you find Kate and her child, summon us immediately. If you don't find them down here, start searching the third level of bedrooms. We'll join you when done on the second floor."

The two scaly giants bowed respectfully. "Yes, your majesty."

"Wait a minute," Romeo said, just before the guards started off on their quest. They paused and stood waiting, their demonic faces impassive.

"Yes, Romeo?" said Jackie, impatiently. "What is it now? You've just pointed out that we're running out of time. We need to get my grandson, and quickly."

"Yes, yes, yes, I'm aware we need the baby. But—aren't we overlooking something?"

Jackie's face twisted up in anger. Surely Romeo wasn't about telling her they'd just had another setback. She'd had enough setbacks for a lifetime already and all of them within the past twenty-four hours. It was

232

unbelievable that so much could go wrong in just one day.

"We still don't know who removed your daughter from the royal castle to here. Or how. Or *why*."

"So? What does that matter? All that matters at the moment is that we know where she and her little brat are. The brat is what's important."

He frowned down at her beautiful face. "Your majesty, whoever did it is very likely still around. They may try to ambush us. We need to be careful. At least until our reinforcements arrive." He bowed. "It would be disastrous for our glorious race if something unforeseen were to happen to you at this advanced stage in our preparations. Please consider that, my dear."

She grudgingly admitted that he was right. "Okay, so we'll be careful. Hmmm, now you've got me remembering, Romeo. Those two policemen I fed on mentioned that someone named Lucy was going to find a baby for them."

"Who's Lucy?"

"I honestly have no idea. I once knew a girl with that name. But she's—oh, forget her—it must be someone else."

Romeo looked worried as he stared darkly around the main foyer of the Madison House, with its stained-glass window stretching upward from the ground floor to the second along the path of the grand staircase. "So we know the kidnapper is a woman then. Most likely a powerful witch."

"She's most likely some friend of Kate's, here with a mistaken idea of rescuing her," Jackie said. "Look, if we find her we'll just sacrifice her too." She paced back and forth testily. "Or I'll empty her veins to calm my nerves."

"I just wonder where she is," Romeo said.

"Romeo, you bloody idiot," Jackie cried in exasperation, baring her glittering fangs at him, "where else could she be, except with Kate and her baby? Now can we just start our goddamn search?!"

***

Lucy Westerna was actually right beside them, listening to their conversation. She was sitting on a period chair by the foot of the stairs.

Before the vampires appeared, the ghost been pondering why she could no longer get into Kate's bedroom. Not like it was a crisis; or rather, it was a crisis, but currently a *minor* one—with the two policemen dead there was no one to give the baby to anyway; no one to sacrifice it.

The *major* crisis Lucy was pondering was how to shut down the vampire's portal. After discovering Detective Vincent's and Bottle's corpses, she'd gone over to their car. There, she'd found Vincent's remote detonator for the explosives. Problem was, there was a lock code on the remote control. Try as she might, she couldn't activate the packages. So, she was stumped, trying to figure her way out of this puzzle.

Now, hearing the bloodsuckers' discussion, she was glad the baby's bedroom was inaccessible. They wanted the baby. And the desperation in the vampire queen's voice and the corresponding look in both she and her warlock's eyes assured Lucy that their plans for Kate's child didn't involve bathing and nursing it.

That certainly is one unfortunate baby, Lucy thought grimly. *Whatever happens tonight, I don't foresee it living through it.*

Romeo Luiz was meanwhile replying the evil queen: "Yes, your majesty. You're right, of course. Guards! Continue on as the queen ordered."

The guards, however, didn't move.

"Well, what are you two waiting for?" the queen snapped at them, her face furious.

One of the eight-foot monsters sniffed the air. The other had his head cocked like a dog. "Two people are approaching us from the front door," the guard said. "They are *good* people. Definitely enemies of ours."

"What!?" Queen and warlock both turned to look in that direction.

When Lucy saw who it was walking towards them, she smiled. Maybe all hope wasn't lost for humanity yet.

"Well, well, well," the vampire queen barked. "Look who's here to save the day. If it isn't Little William and the Creature From the Black Lagoon." Her voice rose to a strident pitch: "Guards, get them. Tear them limb from limb! Paint the walls with their blood!"

As the hulking monsters charged at William and his companion, Lucy tried to be philosophical. True, four against two wasn't exactly great odds, but still, it could have been a lot worse. At least, the rest of the vampires were still back in the Darkness trying to reorganize themselves. No undead reinforcements would be arriving for Jackie Nixon for at least the next few minutes.

235

***

Jay had been right about the house treating them with respect now. They'd had no further trouble from it as they strode through its rooms.

The trouble waited further ahead.

No sooner had William and Jay caught sight of Jackie and her companion as they emerged from the rear hall, then two immense demon guards were charging at them.

William had a moment when he felt like turning and running. It was moments like this that made one question one's faith. Exactly what good were sacred vestments, crosses and holy water against creatures like these? Yes, William had much experience dealing with vampires and other undead, but each new encounter tested him afresh. Particularly now, when he was just-restored to the priestly fold. Would the holy invocations still work? Would the holy water? Would God still honor him in this battle against the forces of Hell? Would the stakes still kill vampires?

But then, the demons were upon he and Jay and the time for reflection was past. The battle for humanity had begun—again!

Their bundle of stakes clattered to the floor. Those were for later, when they fought the vampires.

William discovered he'd not lost his touch. As one of the reptilian monsters swiped at him, he automatically ducked aside; the action came to him naturally, almost like an inborn reflex.

236

The guard's momentum carried it past him. By the time it had spun around to face him again, he'd regained his balance and was holding up a crucifix at it. On seeing the holy relic, the monster covered its face with its claws and backed off. After a sideways glance that showed him Jay squeezing the other demon guard in a bear hug, William stepped forward after his retreating opponent. His free hand now held a bottle of holy water. He splashed this on the demon guard.

"E nominei Christi, I banish you back to Hell where you belong!"

The guard's skin flared up in flames where the holy water struck its body. It screamed in pain as the floor beneath it opened up and engulfed it in a pool of fire. William splashed more holy water on it as, still howling in agony, it sank out of sight. The ground covered it.

William turned around to see the second demon guard being absorbed into the mansion wall against which Jay had thrown it. The monster had a look of utter horror on its face that made William pity it.

I bet it would prefer to have been sent back home like its friend, he thought.

He looked at Jay Cristiano. Jay was cracking his knuckles.

"Let's take on the queen and her boyfriend," Jay said.

This time they didn't wait for the attack to come to them. Howling, they charged at Jackie Nixon and Romeo Luiz.

***

237

Two-on-two's much better odds, Lucy thought. Though impressed by how effectively her young friend from the Melas Industrial Home For Troubled Youth and his badly-scarred companion had dealt with the opposition, she still worried. Though physically impressive, the demon guards could still be considered small fry. The real battle was going to happen now.

***

Jay squared off against Romeo Luiz; William against Jackie Nixon. No one said anything. The time for bravado and posturing was past. This was a conflict of life and death.

***

Jackie Wilson snarled at William. Slowly, she circled him. She was wary of both the crucifix he held and the bottle of holy water. He turned with her, wary of her long sharp claws.

He raised the crucifix and she shielded her eyes against its holy glare. He splashed the holy water at her, but she anticipated its coming and ducked out of the way of the airborne liquid. She skipped back from him, then forward again, trying to get around the holy objects in his hands to land a killing blow. He moved towards her seeking an advantage but was ever wary of her fangs and razor-sharp claws, knowing that all it took was a single bite or slash to tear his throat out. Both of them were conscious of the passage of time. Neither of them could afford its wastage.

238

And so the back and forth motion, the lunging and ducking continued on both sides. Except for the grim expressions on both their faces, an uninformed onlooker could be forgiven for assuming the vampire queen and the young priest were rehearsing a new dance.

***

Teeth bared, hand extended into claws, snarling like a rabid dog, Romeo Luiz immediately leapt at Jay Cristiano. He was going for Jay's throat. Jay grabbed his wrists and forced him back. Romeo freed a hand and ripped Jay's chest open with his claws. Blood spilled. Bloodlust in his eyes, Romeo leaned in for the kill. Jay, however, reading the vampire's deadly intent, quickly head-butted him violently in the mouth. Blood spilling from his split lips, Romeo Luiz stepped back. Jay followed him.

They strained in a contest of strength again, then both toppled to the floor with Romeo landing on top of Jay.

The vampire warlock slowly forced his fangs down towards Jay's throat.

***

Startled by the noise of Jay's fall, William looked over at him. Taking his eyes off of Jackie Nixon was a grave mistake however. His momentary glance barely lasted a second, but it was too long; he'd just given her the opening she needed. Before William could recover his defense, Jackie was upon him.

239

She was a vampire and thus stronger and faster than any human. She was also powered by her desperation. She streaked at him like the wind.

She knocked both the crucifix and bottle of holy water from his hands. The cross clattered away across the room. The water bottle shattered on the tiles, its precious liquid content streaming away across the floor.

William was horrified for a moment, but then Jackie Nixon knocked him half senseless with a hard blow to the forehead.

He slumped to the floor, staring dully up at her as she stalked off to help Romeo Luiz, who at the moment was getting the worse of the fight with Jay Cristiano.

***

Jay now had rolled them both over, so he was on top of the vampire warlock. Focused as he was on his own side of the conflict, he'd not even heard William hit the ground. Besides, he and Romeo Luiz were making too much noise of their own rolling all over the place.

Romeo was still fighting back violently. By now he'd ripped Jay's chest open in three places, in one of which the bloody flesh hung off of Jay's ribs.

However, though racked with incredible pain, Jay fought on relentlessly.

The vampire looked bad too, his nose was squashed flat and blood was gushing both from his nostrils and his mouth. His red eyes were inexorable in their desire to kill his opponent.

Neither of them had tried incantations or invocations in this cramped space. Both were trusting on the superiority of the powers they served—Good versus Evil—to grant them the victory in this fight. In a sense, this was as much a contest of wills as of supernatural forces.

But now, Romeo Luiz made a mistake. Seeing what he believed to be an opening caused by the weakening of Jay's left arm, he lunged up from the floor to sink his teeth into Jay's neck.

But Jay Cristiano had merely been deceiving him. The moment the vampire lunged up off the floor, Jay hit him with a hard elbow to the jaw. Knocked half senseless (almost as bad as William was across the hall) Romeo Luiz fell back to the floor, additionally stunning himself when his head cracked loudly against the tiles.

Then, before Romeo could even begin to recover himself again, Jay Cristiano had pulled two long knives from his belt.

After quickly making the sign of the cross, he slammed one knife into Romeo's chest. Deep into his heart. The second blade he slashed across the vampire's neck.

Romeo let out a single scream of pain as the knife was staked through his heart. He could tell that there was silver in the blades: already he felt the metal's poison ending his life. He stared up in horror at the scarred man who was killing him.

He was still trying to speak, when Jay Cristiano successfully sawed his head off and threw it away across the room.

The vampire warlock immediately crumpled into dust.

***

The moment Romeo Luiz's head hit the far wall and vanished into it was the same moment at which vampire queen Jackie Nixon leapt up on Jay Cristiano's back. As the man staggered up to his feet to fend her off, Jackie Nixon reached around and gouged his throat with her claws. The knife in Jay's right hand clattered to the floor. She ripped across his throat again, then leapt down from his back and quickly slashed him across the eyes. His eyes erupted into messy white pits as her claws tore through them.

Then vampire queen watched the blinded man stagger about for a minute, then, struck by a sudden morbid inspiration, she leaned forward and shoved him hard against the nearest wall.

A moment later, she had the satisfaction of watching William's ugly friend howl and groan in pain as he was sucked up and absorbed into her house.

CHAPTER 33

In the meantime, Lucy had transported herself, first into the Darkness to check on the vampire's progress in reorganizing themselves, then outside into the yard to have a look around.

On the vampire side of things, all was still relative bedlam. The word was spreading that the princess had been found and the ranks of bloodsuckers were reforming, but it was slow. By her calculations, none of the vampires would be arriving in the Madison House for at least ten minutes, maybe fifteen.

Outside the mansion, on the other hand, she'd discovered William and his friend's truck, with its cargo of explosives. The RAM's key was in the ignition (left there at William's suggestion in case their plan flopped and they needed to make a fast getaway). She also realized the truck was wired to blow. This case, however, seemed even less of a help than were all the explosives the two cops had planted around the mansion—this time she couldn't find the detonator for the explosives anywhere. Which meant it would have to be inside the house.

So, she'd teleported herself back inside the house to look for it. She was just in time to see the last of Jay Cristiano—his boots—being sucked into the left wall.

243

William lay stunned on the floor, with blood streaming from his forehead. Jackie Nixon was walking towards him with a determined look on her face. A look that said the young priest was so, so dead.

Retaining her invisibility so neither of them could see her, Lucy did a quick search through William's robes for the detonator. But she couldn't find it anywhere on him.

Shit! she thought. *What the hell do I do now? I need to blow up this unholy place before the vampires arrive. If I can just touch off the explosives in that pickup truck, the resulting blast should be enough to detonate the other explosives placed around the house and make everything*—she looked sadly at William—*and everyone in here go 'boom!' It's so simple—even the evil baby will go up in the blast, completing the required sacrificial chain—and yet it's so damn difficult. Shit! I've got everything I need to save the world except something to start off the damn explosion for me.*

An idea occurred to her: *Matches maybe?* She considered that option, then quickly abandoned it. Her poltergeist abilities were absolutely crap. She wasn't that kind of ghost. (She'd just about managed with the baby upstairs; and that had tested her abilities to the limit.) She'd never be able to strike the matches to start the fire. What she needed was something like a detonator, something that merely required a slight mechanical push to set it off.

But there were none of those about.

Lucy Westerna retired to sit on her previous period chair and ponder this dilemma.

244

Jackie Nixon had by now reached William and was yanking him up to a sitting position while slapping him viciously. Lucy watched their exchange with only half of her mind. She needed to think of a way to blow up the house before the damn vampires got their act together again.

***

William stared blearily into Jackie Nixon's face. His head felt like he was in a bad state of drunkenness. The vampire woman's face and voice both intensified and receded from his senses.

I've failed, he realized. *Jay and I both failed. Now it's all over for everyone. Earth is doomed. The vampires have won.*

He hated thinking like this, but he couldn't help it. There were no cavalry coming to save the day, no cowboys riding in on white stallions to help humanity. It was over. He knew it was. He'd known it when he'd watched Jay Cristiano die, blinded and streaming blood from his throat, eaten by the house; in the end a victim of the very building they'd come to destroy.

It *was* over.

Jackie was smiling at him. Her red eyes gleamed with delight. "So, William, we've won, and you've lost. *Humanity* has lost."

He wished she wouldn't rub it in his face.

"What have you done with Kate?" he asked. "Where is she?" He found it odd that at this moment, with the fate of the entire planet at stake, he was more concerned about the fate of one woman.

She looked at him queerly. "You really do care for her? You still love her? After the way she betrayed you?"

"Yes, I loved her. I still do. She's going to have our child."

Jackie rolled her eyes. "Oh, that." She laughed. Congratulations, priest, you're a daddy. You've got a little baby boy. I don't know how his old Popeness in Rome will take the news, but—"

"Don't sacrifice my child," William pleaded. "Please."

She smirked down at him. "There's no need to do so anymore. Like I said, we've won. You were humanity's last line of defense, William, and you're finished. For good." She gripped his neck and squeezed it painfully till he felt his vertebrae would pop from the pressure of her fingers. "See, Romeo Luiz was going to kill yours and Kate's brat to free the Red Beast of Hell—in a weakened state, mind you—as a distraction to keep you and your dead friend occupied while we started to eat our way through humanity."

"Romeo's dead. God be praised. You can't free the beast anymore."

"Yes, he's dead. But it doesn't matter, does it? With you subdued, I no longer need to free the beast. It'll remain where it belongs, under lock and key. From all accounts, it's too much trouble to let loose." she smiled at him, her tongue licking between her fangs, "At least, not until I've found me a replacement warlock."

Her grip on his throat was excruciating now, and he felt like he'd soon black out, but he forced the words out. "You're crazy."

"I'm victorious."

"Either way, you're still crazy. Just kill me and get it over with then. I'm not afraid to die. I know where I'm going."

She grinned broadly. "Oh no, you don't. See, kiddo, your show of devotion to my daughter and grandson has touched me so immensely that I'm giving you a second chance."

"Huh?" Then, understanding what she meant, a look of disgust and dread spread over his face. "No, no, no!" he grunted, and began struggling feebly in her grasp.

"Yes, yes, yes, Father William," the vampire queen said. "I'm going to turn you into one of us. You got away last time, but not this time. This time you're going to become a vampire and like it. We'll feed on humanity together and you'll love my daughter—who actually does love you too—*I* was the one who demanded that she betray you. And we'll all be one big happy family of vampire royalty." She gestured across the room to the stained patch of floor where Romeo Luiz's clothes lay full of ash. "And you'll be my new warlock. You just need to read up a bit on spells and magical stuff like that. But then, you seminarians are good at studying anyway."

He looked at her, unable to speak. Everything horrible that he'd tried to avoid was coming at him now, as relentless and unstoppable as a freight train.

"Welcome to the Darkness, William," she said. "Now, don't be ungrateful. I'm giving you eternal life. You'll live, together with your wife and child." She smirked. "I'll even force the Pope to perform your wedding."

247

"NOOO!!!" he shrieked as her mouth opened and her teeth descended towards his neck.

Her fangs grazed his neck, just breaking the skin, but then she stopped and began twitching. She let go of him and he scuttled away from her like a startled crab.

God's just granted me a reprieve, but how?

He stared at Jackie Nixon. She was staring back at him, her eyes scared now. Then a change came over her face: its hard lines softened into an expression he recalled from long ago, the facial expression of a dead woman.

"Hello, baby," someone else said through the vampire queen's mouth.

The voice was familiar in its difference, another echo from beyond the grave. "Lucy?" he asked. "Lucy Westerna? How?"

"Yes, Will, it's me." She smiled. "I'm in possession of Jackie Nixon now. I've neutralized her. Now you've got to get out of here."

He thought quickly. "Hold her motionless, while I get a stake."

He leapt to his feet to dash across the hall, but she halted him with a hand on his sleeve. "Stop," she said. "Forget the stake, there's no time for that."

"But *we need* to kill her—for the world's sake." It was weird, talking to Lucy in the vampire queen's body, hearing her reply through the woman's mouth. He was certain Jackie could hear what they were saying; Lucy just had her so powerless that she couldn't do anything.

"Don't bother about killing her. She's going to die anyway. But you know this is bigger than just her, we've got to take out all the vampires."

"Okay, what do you want me to do?"

"I want you to leave. Hurry up. Just get out of the mansion and as far away from it as possible. Leave your truck though, I need it. I already checked, you guys left the car keys in the ignition. Leave them there. Me and the vampire queen here, are going for a short drive."

"Kate and the baby? My son?"

A soft look came over Jackie Nixon's face. "Sorry, Will, but you can't save them. They're a necessary sacrifice to save the world."

"I can't just leave them to die."

She shook her head at him. "You have to, Will." She gestured back at the black opening into the darkness. "Trust me, it's the only way to lock the portal again."

He stared at her. It was horrible to realize what was going to happen. "I have a son and he's going to die! C'mon, Lucy, there has to be something we can do?"

"There isn't. At the moment, this mansion has locked the boy inside one of its bedrooms. Even I can't break into the place." Her voice became urgent. "Now you must go. I can sense the vampire horde approaching. They'll be here in mere moments, and then everything you've so far done will have been for nothing." She extended one of Jackie Nixon's hands towards him and took his hand. Her touch was soft, gentle and soothing. "Come, William, I'll walk outside with you. Once again, I'm sorry, but this really is the only way to save the planet."

Convinced, yet torn inside himself, the priest walked beside the possessed vampire queen out of the Madison mansion. The vampire queen walked with a jerky, zombie motion. She was clearly trying to resist being manipulated. She had no success.

***

Outside, beside the explosive-laden RAM truck, Lucy/Jackie stopped and kissed William gently on the lips.

"Now run, darling," she said. "Get as far from here as you can." She pointed towards the Madison House. "Like I said before when were inside, Jackie and me are going on a short drive. Needless to say, only one of us is gonna survive the trip." She giggled. "Oh, Jackie Nixon, this is gonna be one really explosive party. Oh, it's gonna be quite a blast."

Understanding clearly what she had in mind to do, William nodded. He kissed her once on Jackie's cheek, then turned and set off running down the mansion's driveway, down to where the parked rental car waited.

As he ran, he remembered Jay Cristiano's earlier statement while he'd been wiring the truck to explode. "The Lord works in mysterious ways," Jay had said.

Never were truer words ever spoken, William thought, racing away from the site of danger. *I'd never have foreseen this conclusion to events in a million years.*

CHAPTER 34

Jackie Nixon fought with all her might against the spirit that possessed her. But it was useless, the ghost had iron control over both her will and her body. Now, too late for it to be any use to her, she both knew who 'Lucy' was and how she'd gotten Kate out of the Vampire Castle. She simply 'walked' her out, likely using some ghost ability so that no one saw her.

Jackie Nixon raged in silence. She was helpless, completely neutralized. She did what the ghost made her do. She opened the door of the truck and slid in behind the wheel. She depressed the brake with her foot and switched on the ignition.

No, no, no! her mind shrieked. *It can't end like this! it just can't! Not when I'm so fucking close!*

This last was what hurt Jackie Nixon the most: the fact that all her plans were going to fail right at the finish line. Right when she'd had everything set up for success. It was so unfair! It was also impossible for her to accept that her plans for world dominion were going to fail because of a ghost—an element she'd not even considered at any point.

But that was the painful truth she now had to face: She was finished. Her dream of ruling the vampire world finished for good.

251

"Yee-haa! Let's roll!" she heard herself yell. And then, next, her hand was shifting the gear shaft and her foot pumping the gas pedal.

The deadly truck leapt forward towards the house, but then, at the ghost's urging, Jackie found herself wheeling the vehicle round and heading down the drive. She wondered where they were going now. She'd imagined they were going to crash into the mansion. She'd already seen that the pickup truck was packed high with wired boxes that could only be explosives.

"We don't wanna mess this up, see?" she answered her question in that horrible modulated voice that wasn't her own. "We wanna do this right, don't we, honey?" She giggled excitedly. "And, to do this right, we need to work up a good runway first. Just like an airplane needs to take off."

In the vehicle headlights, she saw the tiny figure of that stupid 'Chosen One' priest fleeing. Oh, how Jackie Nixon hated him. But it was a miserable, powerless hatred. Her main concern now was for her own life. How to save it. Except she could break the ghost's control over her body, she would surely burn to ash when the truck exploded.

She did her best to wrest control of her body from the ghost. Once again, the battle was a waste of time. She could even sense the ghost's amusement at her weak efforts.

Please, Lucy, no! she screamed in her mind. The ghost merely laughed in delight.

As a last desperate resort, Jackie tried to will her foot to stay down on the gas pedal, willing the vehicle to keep going on down the road after the fleeing priest. All she needed was a short respite of time, enough for her vampire forces to emerge from the Darkness and come after her and save her.

With all her mental energies, she tried to keep the truck rolling in a straight line down the road away from her house.

Instead, she found herself spinning it in a tight circle so that it was facing up towards the mansion again.

Noooo! Jackie thought.

There was a pause of maybe a second when she could hear her heartbeat pounding loudly in her ears, and then she heard herself yell in a gleeful voice:

"Alright, Jackie girl, let's roll!"

Then she was flooring the gas pedal again, and holding it down, working to get as much acceleration and speed out of the vehicle as it streaked upward and through the mansion gates towards its darkened destiny.

The ghost was laughing out loud through her. Inside she was weeping and screaming in horror as the building's front wall came ever closer and closer.

"Here we are, baby!" she screamed. "YEAH!!"

And then everything was fire and smoke and violence and pain and the tearing of her flesh and a raging inferno of the like she'd never imagined. Her body exploded and her limbs were torn off her torso. And in the midst of all this Lucy Westerna's ghost exited her, granting her control of her body again, and the dying Jackie Nixon discovered that in truth, death was a very horrible thing.

***

William was half a mile down the road when he heard the first explosion. This was quickly followed by a series of others. He turned back towards the Madison mansion and watched the inferno rage.

After a while, he smiled. It was a smile both of loss and of victory.

"We're safe," he said aloud, knowing in his heart that this was the truth.

***

The first wave of vampires was just arriving at the portal when it shrunk to a pinpoint and disappeared. In addition, the second exit from the darkness, the one into the mansion cellar, vanished at exactly the same time.

It took a long while for the vampires to realize what had happened. When, however, they finally understood that they'd been foiled, that they no longer had any way out of their realm into the human world, they set up a loud frustrated howling.

Finally, the undead retreated back to their castle to plan and scheme. They were immortal after all, they had all the time in the world.

Sooner or later, their time would come, and the necks of mankind would feel the bite of their terrifying teeth.

EPILOGUE

" . . . And so, my brothers and sisters in the Lord, it is imperative that at this time were all keep in mind what this town had been through and resolve to be good citizen of both this earthly realm and the world promised to us with the appearing of our glorious Messiah. Remember with me now the word of our Lord, when speaking to the people of his time He said, 'Render unto Caesar those things that are Caesar's and unto God those things that are God's. And so, I must enjoin you all to..."

While delivering his sermon, the Reverend Father William McConnellson the Third smiled down benevolently at his congregation. The First Catholic Church of Melas was packed from wall to wall. This was a good time, it seemed, to have faith.

The town itself was alive again, most of its primary reconstruction projects either completed or almost so. The late billionairess and philanthropist Jackie Nixon had already provided sufficient funds for a large amount of the required rebuilding. What she hadn't already paid for was handled by private firms eager to invest in the town.

And there were *many* people interested in returning and living in Melas now. Many who'd lived there before the 'vampire scare' and many who discovered Melas afterward. There was just something about Melas now: something 'delightful and wholesome,' something 'sweet and pure' in the air, something that made lots of folks who were just driving through the town on their way elsewhere to decide on the spot: "Yeah, this is the kinda place I want to live in. I'll find an estate agent and enquire about vacant properties for rent."

And so, it went on.

The Moran-Smith Construction Corporation was still handling the rebuilding, under new chairmanship, of course. The state supervisory boards and commission came over from time to time, expressed their deep satisfaction with how the reconstruction was proceeding, and left. The county had voted funds for schools and libraries and there was even talk of establishing a branch of West Virginia University there, after all, there was no longer a Melas Community College since the town had been decimated a few years earlier due to a flood.

Watching his parishioners disperse after evening mass, Father William McConnellson was happy. The young priest was happy most of the time now. Now there was no longer anything to fear when the sun went down.

He'd seen Lucy Westerna just once after the Madison House blew up. On that occasion, she'd assured him that the vampires 'were back were they belonged.' To William's mind, that knowledge was in itself more than sufficient cause for celebration.

Occasionally, when he remembered Natasha Thayer, Kate and the baby, William felt sad. But then he remembered also the Darkness and all those frustrated bloodsuckers once again safety locked away where they couldn't hurt anyone, and he smiled.

Losing these women and his baby boy hurt him a lot, a whole damn lot, but all things considered, for the safety of humanity the trade had been worth it.

The End

CODA

Far away on the other side of Melas, a pair of scientists from the US Geological Survey were studying the now empty lakebed of what once was Floyd Lake. On the hill side above was the blasted knoll of where the Madison House once stood.

The team was onsite because seismic activity had been detected in the area and they were trying to pinpoint its cause.

A massive sinkhole had formed in the center of the lake that reminded them of a drain hole in an oversized bathtub. Completing this analogy was a tiny stream that had once crossed the lake was now spilling into the gigantic hole.

Approaching the rim to study the anomaly, the two could feel an uncanny heat coming from the hole.

"Can't quite see the bottom, Stanley," said Reggie, a man with cropped hair and wire-rimmed glasses announced as he carefully looked over the edge.

Stanley joined him on the precipice. "Hey, do you see something down there?"

Reggie squinted. Suddenly, the earth shifted below his feet and he fell into the sinkhole.

He screamed. As he fell, he kept hoping for a soft landing into some water that did not come. In a free fall, he gasped in horror as a pair of blazing eyes and razor-sharp teeth almost as big as the sinkhole itself of the Red Beast of Hell rushed to meet him.

ABOUT THE AUTHOR

Gary Lee Vincent was born in Clarksburg, West Virginia and is an accomplished author, musician, actor, producer and entrepreneur. In 2010, his horror novel *Darkened Hills* was selected as 2010 Book of the Year winner by *Foreword Reviews Magazine* and became the pilot novel for *DARKENED - THE WEST VIRGINIA VAMPIRE SERIES*, that encompasses the novels *Darkened Hills, Darkened Hollows, Darkened Waters, Darkened Souls* and *Darkened Minds*. He has also authored the bizarro thriller *Passageway*, a tribute to H.P. Lovecraft.

Gary co-authored the novel *Belly Timber* with John Russo, Solon Tsangaras, Dustin Kay and Ken Wallace, and co-authored the novel *Attack of the Melonheads* with Bob Gray and Solon Tsangaras. Both books are in production to be major motion pictures.

260

His short story *Glory Holes* appears in *The Big Book of Bizarro*. His short story *The Tailsman* appears in *Westward Hoes* and was recently made into a comic book by Burning Bulb Publishing's comics division. His short story *Cocaine Connie* appears in the *Night of the Living Dead* tribute anthology *Rise of the Dead*.

As an actor, Gary starred in over fifty feature films and television series, including *My Uncle John is a Zombie!*, *Killer Campout*, *Wrestlemassacre*, *The Walking Dead*, *Stranger Things*, *House of Cards*, and *Mindhunter* to name a few.

As a musician, Gary has produced three CDs: *100 Percent*, *Passion, Pleasure & Pain*, and *Somewhere Down the Road*. A forth musical project, *Passion, Pleasure & Pain 2: The Edge of Forever*, is in the works.

To learn more about Gary Lee Vincent, visit his website at www.garyleevincent.com.

ALSO BY GARY LEE VINCENT

WWW.GARYLEEVINCENT.COM

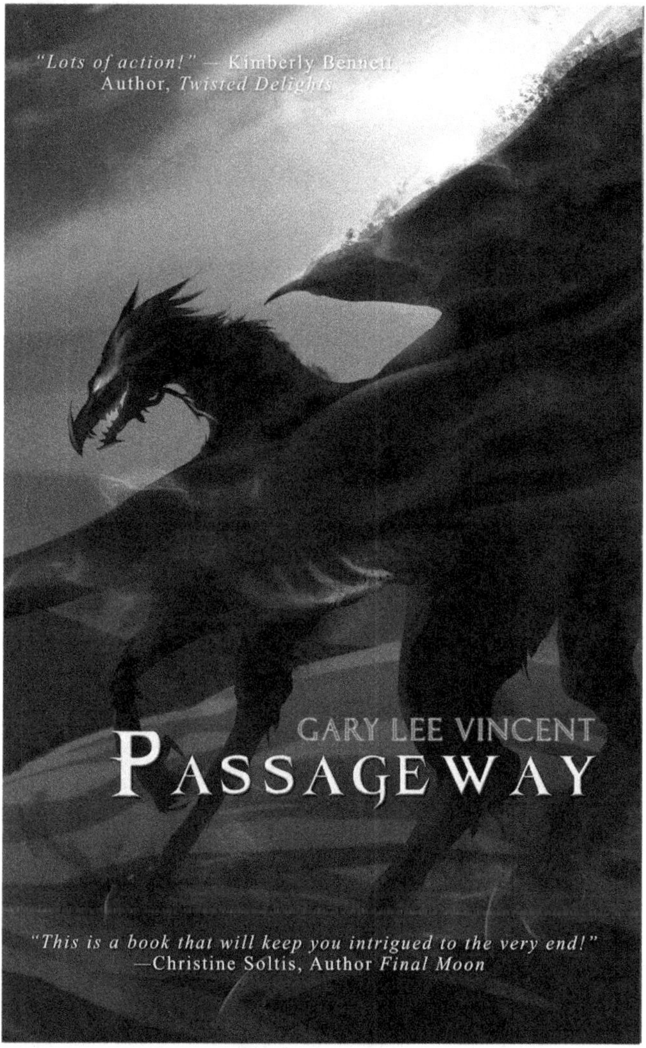

"Lots of action!" — Kimberly Bennett
Author, *Twisted Delights*

GARY LEE VINCENT
PASSAGEWAY

"This is a book that will keep you intrigued to the very end!"
—Christine Soltis, Author *Final Moon*

When an archaeological dig goes horribly wrong, the team is trapped in an alternate world where evil awaits them at every turn. Find out who will survive the Passageway! Skeleton warriors, zombies, other undead beings and werewolves are all very real inside the Passageway! Embark on a deadly tale that will keep you guessing which path to take as you descend into madness in Gary Lee Vincent's bizarro tribute to H.P. Lovecraft. Passageway will leave you breathless to the end!

www.GaryVincent.com
Burning Bulb
PUBLISHING

NOW A MAJOR MOTION PICTURE!

ONE FAMILY'S LEGACY CARVED IN FLESH

BELLY TIMBER

A NOVEL BY
GARY LEE SOLON JOHN
VINCENT TSANGARAS RUSSO

BASED ON A SCREENPLAY BY
KEN WALLACE & DUSTIN KAY

BELLY TIMBER

From the writers of Darkened Hills, Detour to Armageddon and Night of the Living Dead comes a novel unlike any other...

In the 1800's, ordinary people learned the secret of the Kala and undertook extraordinary measures to rid the earth of this evil. This is their story.

For John McCormick, life on the Indiana frontier held nothing but promise. His settlement along the White River would soon become the crossroads of America. Friends and family from back in Ohio and other points east were all making plans to see what all the fuss was about in the newly-formed city of Indianapolis. Yes, things were good. John had his general store and his friend George Pogue had his blacksmith business. Claims were being staked and relations with the native Indians were amicable. The town was growing and nothing could be better... or so he thought.

In Ohio, an evil was brewing. The Lecky Family, a group of ruthless Mongolian nomads, had made their way to America and were practicing their cannibalistic religion of Kala with reckless abandon. No one was safe, not even John McCormick's family.

Burning Bulb
PUBLISHING

Bob Gray's
ATTACK OF THE
MELONHEADS
NOVELIZATION BY
SOLON TSANGARAS & GARY LEE VINCENT

BOB GRAY'S ATTACK OF THE MELONHEADS

"Melonheads is what I love. Give me a body count and gore, but don't forget the laughs. Anytime that I can be reminded of what makes Horror great it is a good thing. Melonheads does that and is something we should all support. Consider it highly recommended."
—Screamsine.us

Fifty years ago, a doctor sought to cure a terrible disease. Hidden from the world, Doctor Malcolm Crowe toiled in the dead of night while the world was sleeping, creating a new breed of mutant—all in the name of science.

Yes, he thought he could cure the sick children. But he was wrong.

Today, the results of his cruel and unconventional experiments have manifested into an evil never before seen.

Now, in Kirtland, Ohio, the town's unsuspecting residents are about to encounter the full onslaught of this unimaginable terror.

Can something be done before it's too late?

Burning Bulb
PUBLISHING

THE TAILSMAN

From the creators of *The Big Book of Bizarro* and *Westward Hoes* comes a new comic unlike anything you have ever seen!

He's hot on the trail, looking for some *tail*...

Sly Franko was a man of the West, a forger of the wild frontier. Like the Country Western song that would be written years after he died, the words, "Faster horses, younger women, and more money," seemed to be the anthem of this horn dog cowboy.

Franko would ride into town on a blazing saddle, find the closest saloon to wet the whistle, belly up to a good card game, and find him a hot-loving hussy to get his cowpoke on with.

However, Sly might have met his match when a visit to bathroom leads to terror and death. Can Sly and his poker buddies solve the mystery before more of the townsfolk are murdered? Find out in this exciting premier issue of *The Tailsman*!

WWW.BURNINGBULBCOMICS.COM

DEMONEYE

Introducing the pilot episode of DEMONEYE. Here, we are introduced to Dekker Collins and the characters of Canvass Pass. Deborah, the town's highly prized 'lady of the night,' is Dekker's informal partner in helping him rid the town of demons, who are becoming all too frequent these days.

Dekker has discovered their weakness, but can he keep the town safe, as the very tool he needs to give him an edge — DEMONEYE — may also destroy him in the process.

As demons take over the Wild West, one man makes a stand in Canvass Pass. That man is Dekker Collins, the Dead Shot. Dekker's secret weapon against the demons – DEMONEYE – may also be his downfall.

WWW.BURNINGBULBCOMICS.COM

GARY LEE VINCENT'S
DARKENED
THE WEST VIRGINIA VAMPIRE SERIES

DARKENED HILLS

When evil descends on a small West Virginia town, who will survive?

Jonathan did not start out his life to become a rambler, it justworked out that way. William was a troubled youth with something to hide. Both were from Melas, a small town tucked away in the West Virginia hills... a town where disappearances are happening more and more frequently.

After the suicide of a wanted serial killer, the townsfolk thought the nightmare was over. But when a centuries-old vampire is discovered they find out the hard way it's just getting started. Dark secrets can only stay hidden for so long and when the devil comes to collect, there will be hell to pay. Can Jonathan and William find a way to stop the vampire before it's too late? Find out in *Darkened Hills!*

DARKENED HOLLOWS

In the heart-stopping sequel to the award-winning *Darkened Hills*, Jonathan and William must return to West Virginia to face possible criminal charges stemming from their last visit to the damned town of Melas, where both had narrowly escaped the clutches of a vampire seethe.

And as livestock start mysteriously getting murdered with all of their blood drained, worried farmers are searching for answers - leaving the local Sheriff and his deputy racing against time to learn the cause before a more violent crime is committed.

Burning Bulb
PUBLISHING

WWW.DARKENEDHILLS.COM

GARY LEE VINCENT'S
DARKENED
THE WEST VIRGINIA VAMPIRE SERIES

DARKENED WATERS

When the world goes to hell, the chosen must arise!

As Talman Cane orchestrates a flood of epic proportions in this third installment of the *Darkened* series the towns of Melas and Tarklin are caught completely off guard by the deluge. Hell-bent on finishing what they started, the evil brothers return to the lunatic asylum to take care of the witnesses and add to the ever-growing army of the undead.

Aided by Lucifer himself and the insane vampire demon Legion, the stage is set to channel all of the forces of hell to come forth. In an all-out race to survive, Jonathan, William, and Amanda soon discover they are up against impossible odds as Lucifer opens the Gateway to Hell, ushering in the zombie apocalypse and the End Times.

Find out who will survive this cosmic battle of the ages in *Darkened Waters*!

DARKENED SOULS

Melas and the Madison House are about to be rebuilt.
True evil is about to be reborne!

Young ex-priest and vampire-killer William is drawn back to the West Virginian town that almost killed him, where his vampire arch-enemy Victor Rothenstein still stalks the earth.

The town of Melas lies destroyed after the battle of the End of Days. But why is wealthy Jackie Nixon so eager to rebuild it using the bone dust of murdered souls?

Terrible evil has visited before, but the Gateway to Hell is about to be reopened in a horrific climax. And this time – it's personal.

WWW.DARKENEDHILLS.COM

Burning Bulb
PUBLISHING

GARY LEE VINCENT'S
DARKENED
THE WEST VIRGINIA VAMPIRE SERIES

DARKENED MINDS

Jackie Nixon intends to become Vampire Queen, but at what blood-drenched cost?

In this continuation to the explosive infernal saga begun in Darkened Souls, newly-turned vampire Jackie Nixon is taking no prisoners. Accompanied by her daughter, Kate, and by the captive vampire lord Victor Rothenstein, Jackie Nixon explores the Darkness. There, she intends to rouse the slumbering vampire race, bound under an ancient curse, and with their help, rule the human world.

But there's a deadly threat to Jackie's plans. Not just William who is trying to stop her, but her own royal ambitions. If Jackie performs the ritual to wake the sleeping vampires the wrong way, she could instead free the Red Beast of Hell, an unspeakable evil that even the undead fear.

DARKENED DESTINIES

With over 45 people missing after Jackie Nixon's party, the mysteries surrounding Melas and the Madison House keep getting darker.

Now, with legions of vampires at her command, can anything or anyone stop her from gaining complete control over all mankind?

The final battle has begun! As the Vampire Queen ascends her throne and sets to unleash the full forces of darkness, the fate of all things good hangs in the balance.

Burning Bulb
PUBLISHING

WWW.DARKENEDHILLS.COM

OTHER GREAT TITLES FROM

Burning Bulb
PUBLISHING

www.BurningBulbPublishing.com

ANTHOLOGIES
BIZARRO AND TRANSGRESSIVE FICTION

THE BIG BOOK OF BIZARRO

The Big Book of Bizarro brings together the peculiar prose of an international cast of the most grotesquely-gonzo, genre-grinding modern writers who ever put pen to paper (or mouse to pad), including:

NIGHT OF THE LIVING DEAD horror writers John Russo & George Kosana; HUSTLER MAGAZINE erotica contributors Eva Hore, Andrée Lachapelle, & J. Troy Seate and established Bizarro genre authors D. Harlan Wilson, William Pauley III, Wol-vriey, Laird Long, Richard Godwin and so many more!

From Alien abductions to Zombie sex, The Big Book of Bizarro contains OVER FIFTY STORIES of the most outrélandish transgressive fiction that you'll ever lay your capricious and curious hands upon!

WESTWARD HOES

Nine outlaw writers rode into town from obscurity to pen nine tantalizing tales of horror and fantasy, and leaving once they branded their own personal marks on the weird western genre and became living legends of the American Frontier experience.

Like drunken Indian scouts, the writers fervidly tracked down and captured the Western genre, tore off its fashionable veneer and ravished its exposed essence.

So belly up to the bar with your favorite soiled dove and enjoy perusing these thrilling tales of Old West debauchery, danger and desire; compiled by the publisher of The Big Book of Bizarro and featuring the bizarro novella *Big Trouble in Little Ass* by Wol-vriey.

Burning Bulb
PUBLISHING

RISE OF THE DEAD

AN EARTH-SHATTERING ANTHOLOGY OF ZOMBIE TERROR

Featuring Stories By:
John A. Russo   Tyson Blue   F.L. Stice   Nelson W. Pyles
Andy Rausch   Stephen Spignesi   R.D. Riley   Zakary McGaha
David J. Fairhead   Gary Lee Vincent   David C. Hayes   Rachel Montgomery
Paul Victor Wargelin   David F. Walker   William Vitka
Rich Bottles Jr.   Douglas Brode

RISE OF THE DEAD - a collection of seventeen tales of unspeakable zombie terror. Featuring a foreword and short story by John A. Russo and the short story *Cocaine Connie* by Gary Lee Vincent!

www.TheJohnRusso.com

Burning Bulb
PUBLISHING

WEST VIRGINIA-THEMED HUMORROROTICA
BY RICH BOTTLES JR.

HELLHOLE WEST VIRGINIA

From the heights of Mothman's perch high atop the Silver Bridge in Point Pleasant to the depths of Hellhole Cavern in Pendleton County, evil lurks within the shadows as the sun sets upon the haunted hills and hollows of West Virginia.

Bizarro author Rich Bottles Jr. blows the coffin lid off horror genre clichés with this tour de force cast of Eco-friendly vampires, beach-yearning zombies and sex-starved she-devils.

LUMBERJACKED

If you are easily offended or do not possess a truly depraved sense of humor, this story may not be the light summer reading fare you desire. As for the four feisty female freshmen stranded on top of West Virginia's third highest mountain, they have no choice but to experience the sick, twisted debauchery and perverted mayhem described deep inside the tight unbroken bindings of this horrific missive.

Lumberjacked takes the reader to a nightmarish world where character development and aesthetic integrity are prematurely cut short by the swinging axes of maniacal lumberjacks, who are hell bent on death and destruction in the remote forests of Appalachia. And at the climax, when paranoia crosses over to the paranormal, Lumberjacked makes Deliverance look like a family raft trip down the Lower Gauley.

THE MANACLED

What happens when twin brothers lease out the former West Virginia State Penitentiary with the false purpose of filming a documentary on supernatural phenomena, but their true intention is to make a pornographic movie?

Chaos ensues as the disturbed spirits of murdered convicts, along with the reanimated dead from the neighboring Indian Burial Mound, take their vengeance on the unwary and undressed trespassers.

Zombies, ghosts, mobsters and porn collide in this bizarro tale from horror author Rich Bottles Jr.

Burning Bulb
PUBLISHING

WEST VIRGINIA-THEMED HUMORROROTICA

BY RICH BOTTLES JR.

BY

A collection of short stories from Rich Bottles Jr. Be forewarned that the graphic sex and violence described in this book of bizarre short stories may provoke psychological or emotional triggers for some unstable or weak-minded readers, including, but not limited to, the following extreme content: Rape, Torture, Murder, Mayhem, Kidnapping, Cannibalism, Necrophilia, Poisoning, Prostitution, Pornography, Nazis, War Crimes, Ethnic Cleansing, Terrorism, Incarceration, Bondage & Discipline, Sadomasochism, Corporal Punishment, Foot Fetishism, Masturbation, Alcoholism, Drug Abuse, Eating Disorders, Domestic Violence, Mental Illness, Suicide, Drowning, Religious Intolerance, The Occult, Adult Language, Homosexuality, Sodomy, Unwanted Pregnancy, Amputees, Adultery, Incest, Shoplifting, Bukkake, Penis Envy, Cigarette Smoking, and Heavy Metal Music.

THE VAMPIRE WHO SAVES CHRISTMAS

Cantankerous demon Krampus is out to ruin Christmas for everyone, but Mrs. Claus and Jolly Ole Saint Nicholas will do everything in their power to stop his diabolical plan, even if it means becoming vampires to fight the evil villain! Join Alfie the Elf, Rudolpho the Reindeer Trainer, and all the other merry residents of Christmasland in this hilarious yuletide adventure that is sure to become a joyous holiday classic!

THE TAILSMAN

He's hot on the trail, looking for some tail! Follow the adventures of Sly Franko in this ornery comic book set in the *Westward Hoes* universe by Gary Lee Vincent, Rich Bottles Jr., and Stuart Brown.

Burning Bulb
PUBLISHING

WOL-VRIEY
BIZARRO AND TRANSGRESSIVE FICTION

BRAINCHEW

It was supposed to be a simple jewel heist, but it went badly wrong. Chuck got shot and died.

Lance hid his friend's corpse in the Pleasant Street Cemetery. But that was a big mistake—there was something undead, something extremely hungry . . . something eXXXtremely horrible, buried in the Pleasant Street Cemetery.

And Lance had just woken it up.

They called the monster Brainchew because it ate brains. Human brains. And it preferred those brains fresh from the heads . . . of the living.

And now it was awake again, Brainchew planned on feeding big-time tonight. Oh hell yes, it did.

BRAINCHEW 2: OUT OF THEIR HEADS

After Tiff Hooper recognizes Josh Penham, the man who abducted her and kept her in his basement and abused her, she brings her three friends to Raynham for a night of well-deserved revenge on him.

Only things don't go according to plan.

It is never a good idea to leave a corpse in Raynham's Pleasant Street Cemetery. You run the very real risk of awakening what lies underground there. And that thing—Brainchew—is more horrible and more evil than anything the average mind conceives of even in its worst nightmares.

Brainchew is back! And this time the monster is extra-hungry. But there are plenty of delicious human brains about tonight, and Brainchew intends to eat them all before dawn.

Burning Bulb
PUBLISHING

www.ingramcontent.com/pod-product-compliance
Lightning Source LLC
Chambersburg PA
CBHW070855180626
46817CB00003B/779